CONFLICT OF LOVE

Cathy enjoys her job as nanny to six-year-old Jamie Hargreaves, but she thinks that his father, David, who is a widower, takes her too much for granted. Then she meets the rugged, good-looking Rob Tregarth, who lives on a boat on the canal, and they fall in love. But when David has a car accident and it seems he will never walk again, Cathy knows her loyalty lies with him and Jamie. Can she find a solution — and lasting happiness?

Books by Chrissie Loveday
in the Linford Romance Library:

REMEMBER TO FORGET
TAKING HER CHANCES
ENCOUNTER WITH A STRANGER
FIRST LOVE, LAST LOVE
PLEASE STAY AWHILE
A LOVE THAT GROWS

CHRISSIE LOVEDAY

CONFLICT OF LOVE

Complete and Unabridged

LINFORD
Leicester

First published in Great Britain in 2003

First Linford Edition
published 2005

British Library CIP Data

Loveday, Chrissie
Conflict of love.—Large print ed.—
Linford romance library
1. Love stories
2. Large type books
I. Title
823.9′14 [F]

ISBN 1–84395–563–6

Published by
F. A. Thorpe (Publishing)
Anstey, Leicestershire

Set by Words & Graphics Ltd.
Anstey, Leicestershire
Printed and bound in Great Britain by
T. J. International Ltd., Padstow, Cornwall

This book is printed on acid-free paper

1

'Jamie, get off the gate, now, please,' Cathy yelled at her six-year-old charge, as he clambered precariously over the canal lock. 'If you fall in, you're on your own. I'm not going into that foul water for you or anyone else, do you hear?'

'But there's a boat coming. Can't I watch it, Cathy, please? We don't have to go home for ages yet.'

Jamie smiled his sweetest smile at her and immediately she gave in. He could twist her round his little finger.

'Five minutes, and that's your lot. Your dad will be home and then I've got to go to my own home. I do have a life of my own, you know.'

'Glad to hear it,' a man's voice called.

Cathy looked round. She could see no-one but the voice sounded very close.

'Down here, other side of the lock,'

the voice said again.

'Have you got one of the special keys to open the lock?' Jamie asked.

'Certainly have. Are you going to help me, young man?'

'Wow. Yes, please. I can, can't I, Cathy?' he wheedled.

'I suppose, but don't take too long. I really do mean it.'

But her words were lost. The red-headed little boy was already leaping down to the ground and holding a hand out to the man on the narrow boat.

'Don't you dare to drop it in the water,' the man ordered laughingly, 'or I'll hang you over the side by your feet and you'll jolly well grope in the mud till you find it. I don't think your mother will be very pleased.'

He smiled up at Cathy as he spoke. He was good-looking in a rugged sort of way. He could have done with a shave, and his brown hair was distinctly curling round the collar of his ancient, baggy sweater. The bright blue eyes smiled, crinkling at the corners and he showed very white teeth between the stubble.

'She's not my mum,' Jamie screeched. 'She's Cathy.'

'So, Cathy, can this young man help me with the lock? It's very hard work and I'm all on my own.'

He pulled a sad-looking face that made Cathy laugh out loud. She grinned.

'OK, as long as it doesn't take too long and that he doesn't fall in.'

'Guaranteed,' the man said with another smile. 'Rob Tregarth,' he added.

'Cathy Jones,' she introduced herself.

He leaped out of the boat and followed Jamie to the winding mechanism to open the lock. He had already fitted the handle into the right place and was trying to turn it.

'Hold on, there,' Rob called out.

'It's all right. I can do it,' Jamie protested, his face red with his exertions.

'Not with the catch still fixed.'

Rob laughed. He leaned past the child, flicked the well-oiled catch back and helped Jamie to winch open the paddles. The water began to rush into the lock and gradually, the boat rose. Cathy watched with interest as the boat came level with the top of the lock. The deck was clean and tidy with bright flowers in painted tubs. She noticed several types of herb growing in a gro-bag farther down the deck. Inside the window, she could see the living cabin, bright with colourful woven rugs. It looked welcoming and cosy.

'You can go inside if you like,' Rob suggested, seeing her interest.

'Oh, I couldn't, really. I'm sorry. I didn't mean to be nosey. It all looks so pretty.'

'Go on,' he encouraged. 'I'm very proud of my Lady Barbara.'

Not waiting for a personal invitation, Jamie was already climbing into the boat and peering through the doors.

'Wow! You've got a kitchen and

everything. It's really neat. Come on, Cathy. Look.'

Shyly, she climbed down from the tow-path. She stepped inside and echoed Jamie's words.

'Oh, it's great! It's so compact and homely. It's lovely.'

The tiny kitchen, or galley she supposed it should be called, was well-ordered. The whole of the interior was panelled with warm pine and the little, round, brass portholes gleamed brightly. Old-fashioned wall-lamps were hung along the sides and a wood-burning stove sat neatly in one corner. Large, comfortable floor cushions made extra seats, opposite the bench that she assumed doubled as a bed.

'Really, really nice,' she added after gazing round.

'Thank you,' Rob said with a grin, leaning on the door frame and peering into the cabin.

He was tall and looked almost too large for the available space.

'If you'd like to wait till I've cleared

the lock, I'll make you a cup of tea. I was about to have one myself.'

'Thanks,' Jamie said. 'Cool. Can I stay here while you drive through the lock?'

'Once we're through the rise, we have to get right out of the way in case anyone else comes along and wants to go through. I'm going to motor along to the next bridge and then we can moor for as long as we want.'

'We really should be getting back,' Cathy said doubtfully.

Truth to tell, she was captivated by the boat and not entirely disinterested in its owner. Rob Tregarth seemed to be a most unusual man.

'Surely ten more minutes won't hurt. I'd be glad of some company. I'll even let you put the kettle on.'

His eyes sparkled as he spoke and his ready smile was most engaging.

'Well, OK, if you're sure. Jamie would love it, even if it's only a few minutes.'

He nodded and led Jamie outside on

to the small deck. He was busily instructing him and gesturing at the ropes tethering the boat to the side of the lock. Jamie struggled to untie the wet ropes and, helped by Rob, looked very pleased with himself when it landed in the boat. She watched the man and boy for a few minutes, thinking how well Rob communicated. She pushed away the thought, compared to David, Jamie's father. She went back into the cabin.

In the galley, everything was in perfect order. Mugs were standing on a shelf, behind a rail, so they could not slip off if the going was rough. Spoons were arranged neatly in a smooth-running drawer. She opened a cupboard and found coffee. She spent a moment or two looking at the contents of the cupboard. Her mother always said you could learn a lot about a person from the contents of their cupboards. Apart from a lot of spices and dried pulse foods, beans, lentils and such like, and a quantity of canned foods, she could actually learn very little. He was obviously very organised and self-sufficient.

The engine droned on as they travelled along the canal, towards the next bridge. She went outside the cabin to watch. The engine slowed and stopped and the boat continued to move forward. Rob pushed the tiller over and they drifted towards the bank.

'OK, Jamie,' he called, 'jump on to the bank, now.'

The child jumped and promptly fell over.

'Well done, but where's the rope? You were supposed to take it with you.'

Cathy was laughing as the boy stood up crossly.

'Stop laughing at me. I dropped it. How'm I s'posed to jump holding a rope?' he said tearfully.

'It doesn't matter,' Rob called. 'Throw it to him, Cathy.'

She bent down to pick up the soggy end and tossed it towards Jamie. He stood with hands outstretched, waiting.

As he grabbed it, and promptly sat down again in the wet grass, they all laughed. He clung to the rope as if he were tethering some wild beast, until Rob made an easy stride off the boat. He showed the boy how to fix the rope to a post sticking out of the bank.

'Right, you go and tie the other end the same way. There's a ring there, set in concrete.'

Beaming with delight at the responsibility, Jamie trotted to the other end and tied the rope to the ring.

'I'll go down and make that coffee, or do you prefer tea?' Rob suggested.

'I found the coffee already,' Cathy told him.

Rob made the drinks and poured some orange juice from the little fridge for Jamie. The two were sitting on the edge of the boat when he came out with the mugs on a small, brightly-painted tin tray. They all sat peacefully, listening to the gentle lapping of the water.

'So, are you on holiday?' she asked.

'No, though my parents might

dispute that statement.'

'How do you earn your living then?' she asked curiously.

'So far this year, I've picked flowers, fruit and done some hay-making. That was a total disaster, by the way. I got hay fever and spent the next week sneezing, streaming and wheezing. I left that area in rather a hurry.'

'I see.' Cathy laughed. 'And what's next?'

'That's also a matter for discussion. I'm the family black sheep, you see. My destiny should be a suit, collar and tie and to join the family firm. I am supposed to be an accountant. But all that, well, it's not for me.'

Cathy giggled. He certainly looked far from the conventional accountant.

'So, what exactly did you do instead, to make you a family black sheep?'

'Squandered my grandfather's inheritance on buying this boat and trying to follow my dreams.'

'Living on a boat is just about the coolest thing ever,' Jamie shrilled, bouncing up and down on the side. 'I'm going to ask Dad to get us one.'

'And where is your dad?' Rob asked.

'He's at work, busy being a boring old accountant, like you didn't want to be.'

Jamie's open gaze made Rob laugh. His eyes held many more questions. Like where's your mother? But he kept it to himself, not wanting to upset the boy.

'We'd better be getting back, Jamie,' Cathy interrupted. 'Your dad will worry if we're late. Get all the police out on a search party.'

'Cool,' Jamie yelled. 'That would be great fun. The best.'

'Oh, no, it wouldn't, my lad. Come on. Thank Rob for the drink.'

Cathy tried to look strict.

'I don't want to go. Dad'll only be cross and tired, like always.'

'You could always come back tomorrow. I'm thinking of staying here for a while,' Rob suggested.

'Aw, neat,' Jamie screeched. 'I finish

school at quarter past three. We can be here by half past and if we tell Dad we'll be late, we can stay for ages.'

'Jamie, really! Maybe Rob doesn't want us here for ages.'

Rob was staring at Cathy so intently that she blushed.

'I'd actually be very glad of your company,' he said softly.

'Well, if you're sure. Jamie is a noisy little imp at times.'

She very much wanted to take up Rob's invitation and spend some time getting to know this interesting man. Her mind jolted her back. How could she be thinking this way? She was supposed to have given her heart to another, however foolish it may be. She'd been carrying a torch for David, Jamie's father, for as long as she had worked for him, or so she thought.

'See you tomorrow,' Jamie called, leaping off the boat and yet again, landing on his bottom in the wet grass.

'Till tomorrow,' Rob said, taking her hand for slightly longer than necessary.

She nodded and walked up to the bridge after Jamie.

David's car was just stopping outside the house as they arrived back.

'It was great, Dad,' Jamie said excitedly, as Cathy handed him over.

The immediate, excited account of the short time spent on Rob's boat sounded like a major adventure in the Amazon.

'And he says we can go back tomorrow. It doesn't matter if supper's late, does it? Then we can sail along the canal a bit.'

David Hargreaves sighed, as he usually did when Jamie chattered on about his day.

'Calm down, Jamie. Let me get changed at least, before you go into any further details. Do you want to get off home, Cathy?'

'It's OK. You go and change. I'll put the oven on for your meal.'

She watched the tall, distinguished-looking man as he went upstairs. He was always immaculate, never a hair out of place. His serious grey eyes always looked sad and weary and she longed to comfort him in some way. Jamie obviously took after his mother, as he bore very little resemblance to his father. Somehow, there always seemed to be something lacking in the relationship between father and son. It was almost as if the boy made David feel sad.

Cathy had often fantasised that they might have a proper, romantic relationship one day, but as she came to know David better, her hopes had begun to waver. It seemed he was utterly devoted to the memory of his young wife, who had died very soon after Jamie's birth. It must have been a terrible tragedy for them all. Fortunately, Jamie had been much too young to remember his mother, and his father too old to allow himself to forget her. Cathy had looked after Jamie for over four years now and was the nearest thing he had ever had to a mother.

Though she had often thought of

moving on, if only to save her unrequited longing for David, Cathy hadn't the heart to leave Jamie. He would be devastated. In fact she prided herself that it was her influence that had made him such a relatively normal little boy.

She knew in her heart that she should pack away her imaginings and concentrate on someone who might at least reciprocate her feelings. David was apparently unavailable. However much she tried to do for him and Jamie, she recognised that despite her loyalty she was still nothing more than a paid nanny. Admitting to herself that she felt attracted to Rob had to be a step forward.

Even that was pretty stupid, she muttered to herself. He's literally a ship passing in the night. She should not allow herself to wallow in such ridiculous imaginings, especially after just one short meeting.

'I can't wait to go on Rob's boat again, can you?' Jamie said excitedly.

She stared at him. He seemed to have been reading her mind.

'We'll see, Jamie. You go and wash your hands and help Daddy to set the table.'

'I wish you'd stay for supper as well. Then Daddy won't be so cross.'

His face looked crestfallen but Cathy was not impressed. He had tried all sorts of games with her and with his father, poor little boy.

He must often feel confused, she thought.

Sometimes, she felt that David almost blamed the child for his mother's death. It seemed sometimes as if he resented Jamie, the child whose life had cost him his beloved wife. That was the impression Cathy had formed, anyhow.

'I have to go, love. You know I do. You'll have fun with Daddy. Perhaps he'll have a game with you. Ludo or something.'

'He doesn't believe in games that don't teach me something, and I can't do Trivily Suits. That's the only one he likes.'

'You mean Trivial Pursuit, I think. But, of course, Daddy will play something you like. Have you asked him?'

'Nah. He'll have homework to do anyhow. I 'spect I'll just have to watch television, as usual.'

As he went off to wash his hands, Cathy frowned. Maybe there was a grain of truth in his words. David undoubtedly did his best, however much it left to be desired. But he should be able to find just a little bit of time for his son, surely?

2

When she collected Jamie from school the following afternoon, he was bouncing with excitement.

'We are going to see Rob, aren't we? I wrote it in my class diary today, about going on the boat, I mean. My teacher said it was very good.'

Cathy walked along, holding the child's hand, listening to his chatter. Though she dared not admit it to anyone, least of all Jamie, she, too, was feeling just a little excited. Perhaps it was simply because it was something different to do, another adult to chat with. It made a change. The fact that he was an attractive, interesting male was beside the point, she tried to convince herself. Her own social life was seriously lacking, whatever she may have said to Jamie about having a life of her own.

'Hi, glad you could make it,' Rob called from his boat as they joined him later. 'Come on board and we'll have us a bit of a cruise. You ready with the mooring rope, Jamie?'

The child went pink with pleasure at the responsibility and importantly untied the rope.

'What have I got to do?' he asked.

Rob pointed to the front deck and Jamie threw it on. Then the little boy ran back to the rear and leaped on board scared in case they left without him. Expertly, Rob untied the stern mooring, gave the boat a shove from the side of the bank and leaped on board in one easy action. He took the tiller and steered them into midstream.

'That was clever,' Cathy said. 'You've done that a few times.'

'Certainly have. What else when you're both captain and crew? Don't believe anyone who tries to tell you I live a lazy life. A couple of days on board and you'd soon see what hard work it is. Now, if you put the kettle on,

I'll make sure this lad gets a life-jacket.'

He delved into a locker and pulled out a couple of small life-jackets, selected one and fastened Jamie into it.

'Now, you can go more or less where you like. All the same, I don't recommend falling in. The water's pretty murky all around here, and I want to fasten this clip to the rope that goes along the top of the boat. That means you won't slip off the boat. At least we've done our best to stop you drowning.'

'I can swim, you know,' Jamie said indignantly. 'Well, I can, with arm bands.'

'Good for you,' Rob said with a note of admiration in his voice that was not lost on the little boy. 'But we feel happier knowing you are safe, so do as I ask.'

'No probs,' Jamie agreed cheerfully. 'I'm a bit like a dog on one of those long leads.'

Smiling and wishing Rob could be around more often to organise Jamie,

Cathy went into the little cabin and put on the kettle. It was a bit like the caravan holidays she and her brother had shared when they were children. She collected everything together, surprised that the boat seemed to be so steady, even though they were travelling along. She took the drinks up on deck when they were ready. Sipping the hot tea, they motored slowly along the back-water. The gentle throb of the engine was comforting and birds dipped and dived across their route.

It was very peaceful and Cathy felt totally at ease with her new-found companion. She discovered that he was a little older than her twenty-five years, and that he was neither married nor attached to anyone. She felt oddly pleased at this bit of information though she didn't know why she should. After all, he was obviously a wanderer and she was unlikely ever to see him again, once he left the area.

'Do you want to steer?' he asked, when they had finished their drinks.

He was leaning comfortably against the back of the boat, his arm giving the gentlest of nudges to the tiller when needed.

'Oh, I couldn't. I know nothing about boats. I wouldn't know where to start.'

'Come on. Nothing to it. I'll help.'

He pulled himself upright and took her hand, placing it firmly on the tiller. Then, moving round her, he made room for her to stand where she could see the way ahead. She was very pleased that he didn't remove his hand from hers. It was warm and comforting, leaning against his strong body. He was several inches taller than her and she felt protected and safe.

'Move the tiller just a little way, left if you want to turn to the right and the opposite for left.'

'It's very confusing,' she complained. 'I knew I'd be hopeless. I don't even know my right from my left in the first place and that's just going in one direction. Boats are something else entirely.'

Rob laughed, his blue eyes shining with merriment.

'I suspect that must be a girl thing,' he said. 'You're doing fine. I'll just go and check on young Jamie. Won't be long.'

To her horror, he dived into the cabin and disappeared from her sight.

'Rob? Rob, where are you?' she yelled. 'Don't do this to me. I'm going to crash the thing. Help!'

Dratted man. He was deliberately ignoring her.

'Rob, please,' she shrieked, in a panic.

When he still didn't come, she really did panic. It must be Jamie. Something was seriously wrong. David would never forgive her if anything happened to his son. Something must have happened to him and they hadn't even noticed. How could she have been so foolish? She was so busy enjoying herself that she'd forgotten her responsibilities. What would she say to David?

She looked around the little cockpit. There must be a way to stop this thing without having an engineering degree. There was a sort of handle, which obviously turned in both directions. Maybe that was it. She pushed it tentatively and the engine speeded up. She quickly slammed it back the other way and the engine died altogether. Muttering things about irresponsibility and desertion of duty, she tried to steer towards the bank. Immediately, the boat seemed to point straight at the bank and she pushed the tiller back the other way. For such a large, cumbersome thing, it moved remarkably easily and they were back out in midstream.

She tried to push it back more gently this time. They were still moving at quite a speed and again, she feared they were in danger of ramming the bank. She pushed the tiller just a little and the boat swung out again. Once it was parallel to the bank, she straightened it and to her immense relief, it drifted slowly to a halt. Rob's face appeared from the cabin. He'd pulled on a ridiculous woolly cap.

'What's up?' he asked.

'Where on earth were you? Leaving me like that!' she began to protest. 'You're an idiot. Where's Jamie? Is he all right? I was worried when you'd gone for so long.'

'He's fine. Everything's fine. After a few unscheduled wiggles, you managed to stop like an expert. Couldn't have done better myself. But why did you stop?'

'Because you'd disappeared for so long and there was a bend coming up and I thought there must be something wrong with Jamie.'

She continued to feel angry but gradually, she calmed down. He explained carefully that if he hadn't left her alone, she would never have got the feel for the boat.

'You'd have kept asking me what to do all the time. This is the only way, not that I didn't enjoy helping you,' he added. 'Best excuse I know to get close to anyone.'

'And I suppose you get close to lots of people, do you?'

Cathy's eyes flashed in anger.

'Oh, thousands, I guess, but only the pretty ones.'

He had a very wicked grin, she decided, and she simply couldn't be angry for long. He was much too nice.

'I s'pose you're right,' she admitted grudgingly.

'Can I drive now?' Jamie requested, peering up from below.

'I think you'll need a box to stand on,' Rob said. 'If I can find something, you can have a go but you'll have to have help. It's a big, heavy old boat and maybe too much for you to hold on your own.'

'But I'm very strong for my age. Cathy says so,' he protested.

Five minutes later, they were on the move again and Cathy left the two males to it. She went through the cabin and out on to the front deck. There were several cushions placed along the sides. She sat back and stretched her legs. It was certainly very relaxing, being a passenger, at least.

'Lock ahead,' Rob called. 'All hands on deck.'

'Maybe we ought to leave, before you go through it,' Cathy called back. 'Then we won't delay you.'

'Oh, no,' Jamie yelled. 'It isn't a proper trip without at least one lock.'

'But we shall have an even longer walk home.'

'We can always turn round and go back again,' Jamie suggested with an air of triumph. 'Can't we, Rob?'

Rob explained that it wasn't very sensible to use a lock twice, as it wasted a lot of water.

'It's always raining, anyway, so there's masses of water,' Jamie protested. 'Please can we stay, Cathy? The lock is the best bit.'

'OK,' she agreed. 'But no moaning when you have farther to walk home.'

Undeniably, she was very pleased to

spend a little longer in the company of this man. She felt attracted to him, in a way that surprised her. What she felt for Rob was quite different to her imagined love for David. Silly to feel anything, she told herself. She was so very inexperienced, she thought gloomily. At her age, she should know better.

The business of the lock was accomplished smoothly and efficiently.

'You make a fine crew,' Rob said after they had motored a little farther on. They both smiled their pleasure.

'How do you have a bath and well, you know, go to the toilet and everything?'

'There's a proper bathroom if you count a shower, and my bedroom's at the back. You pass it along the little corridor to the cockpit. Go and look if you like.'

Cathy and Jamie went together. It was all perfect, if a little cramped.

'I hadn't realised it was all so organised,' she said. 'It's lovely. Look, I'm sorry, but we really must make a move. Jamie's dad will be furious if we're not back when he gets home,' Cathy said, not a little regretful, but despite all his protests, Jamie was unbuckled from his life-jacket.

'What time do you finish your duties?' Rob asked. 'I mean, would you like to go for a drink this evening, maybe have a bite to eat?'

'Oh,' Cathy replied stupidly. 'I mean, I don't know.'

'Sorry. I sort of got the impression there wasn't anyone in your life. A relationship, I mean.'

'Not really. Well, no, there's no-one.'

She clenched her fists as she spoke. She may have had hopes, but David was still too busy mourning his wife's death.

'No. There's no-one special,' she said firmly.

'I'm glad,' Rob said softly. 'Where shall I meet you? Is there somewhere in the village? I am limited to where I can take you, not having a car or anything.'

'I've got a car. I could drive down to

the bridge near the lock, about half seven?'

'Sounds great,' Rob agreed. 'See you later.'

Cathy and the boy walked home as fast as possible. For once, David had come home early and was in a foul mood.

'Where on earth have you been? I was worried to death. I don't like you being out this late.'

He was already holding a glass in his hand and she recognised the smell of whisky.

'I'm sorry. We did mention it last night.'

Cathy was apologetic, though slightly irritated.

'We've been on Rob's boat. He let me drive and went through a lock an' I turned the handle to open the paddles. Rob told me all about the lock and how it works.'

Jamie's voice was shrill with excitement.

'You see, you start at the beginning

and when the doors are closed . . . '

'OK, Jamie, that's enough. I've got a splitting headache and I have to go out this evening.'

David drained his glass and immediately re-filled it. Cathy looked disapprovingly.

'You can babysit this evening, can't you?' he added.

'She's going out with Rob,' Jamie chimed in, 'the man who has the boat, so she can't, can she? Who'll come to stay with me?'

'Cathy? You can't go out. I need you here. I can't get out of this meeting. You can surely put off your date for once.'

David sounded slightly scornful at the word date.

'Actually, no, I can't. I've no way of letting him know.'

'Didn't even think you knew any boatmen. What sort of date with a boatman can possibly be so important? Bit beneath you, isn't it?'

'How dare you?' she burst out

angrily. 'Rob is polite, decent and very intelligent.'

'He's an accountant, like you, Daddy,' Jamie added. 'Only he's a black sheep as well.'

Cathy stifled a grin. David glared and muttered something uncomplimentary about accountants. He always relied on Cathy, usually so reliable, always willing to take care of Jamie night and day, usually with little or no warning. He had never given a thought to any social life she might have. He supposed she was a reasonably good-looking girl and, well, she even had a nice figure. Perhaps he should have expected that she would have the occasional boyfriend. But it left him with more than a bit of a crisis. He must attend his meeting this evening. He was taking an important client out for a working dinner. The fact that she was a glamorous, youngish woman had only partially influenced his invitation.

'Look, I can't get out of this. Can't you take Jamie with you? Put him to bed on the boat or something?'

'Oh, for goodness' sake, David. He's got school tomorrow. Besides, we're going out for a meal. There has to be someone else you can ask.'

Cathy would normally have given in but for once, she stuck to her plans and refused to budge. David took too much for granted. He emptied his glass for a second time and reached for the bottle.

'I hope you don't intend to drive,' Cathy said quietly.

'You're neither my wife nor my nursemaid,' he snapped. 'Don't try to tell me what I can and can't do. I had enough of that with Hazel.'

He stopped suddenly and bit his lip, glancing at his son. Jamie looked as if he might cry and Cathy looked totally shocked. It was the first time David had ever mentioned his late wife in anything but glowing terms. She'd always believed that Hazel was utterly perfect and they were blissfully happy. Otherwise, why did he always seem so bereaved?

'Sorry,' he mumbled. 'Will you at least give Jamie his meal and put him to bed, before you go out on your evening of delights?'

David could sound very sour at times, she decided.

'OK, but I must leave soon after seven. I must have time to change.'

'I'll have to get on the phone and see if I can make some rescue plans for my evening,' he muttered and went upstairs.

'OK, young man, what shall we find for your supper?'

She offered the perennial favourite, fish fingers and chips, which Jamie loved but didn't have too often, especially when David was around. He disapproved of such instant meals. The child was soon finished and ready for his bath. He was strangely quiet, subdued by his father's outburst, no doubt.

'Dad won't leave me by myself, will he? I don't really mind being on my own but I might be a bit scared.'

‘Of course he won’t. If he can’t find anyone, I’ll just have to go and find Rob and tell him I can’t see him after all.’

‘That’d be a shame. Rob’s nice, especially for an accountant. Dad’s an accountant but Rob isn’t a bit like Dad, is he? He’s much more fun.’

‘An accountant, did you say? Who is?’

David joined in as he came back into the room. With a glare at Cathy, he smiled down at the boy.

‘We told you. Cathy’s boyfriend.’

‘Maggie from the office is coming over to look after you. You like her, don’t you?’ he said as if he hadn’t heard Jamie’s reply.

‘She’s all right,’ Jamie agreed.

Maggie was David’s secretary, a middle-aged spinster who adored her boss and allowed Jamie to twist her round his little finger. She was totally unused to children but would do anything to please David.

‘S’pect I’ll be asleep most of the

time. I'm shattered after this afternoon. It was the business though, wasn't it, Cathy?'

Cathy laughed at his choice of words, relieved that David had sorted everything.

All the same, it was almost a quarter to eight by the time she reached the lock bridge. She had had a quick shower and her long blond hair was still slightly damp. She'd changed into a long, floaty skirt in a deep sea-green colour, with a matching T-shirt. Rob was leaning against the old brickwork, watching the water as it drifted by. She went to stand by him. He had changed into a light denim shirt that matched his eyes perfectly.

'Hi,' he said lightly. 'You look nice. I was beginning to think you'd changed your mind.'

'Sorry, slight problem with Jamie's father. He expected me to hold the fort while he went out, as usual,' she said a trifle snappily.

'I see. So what happened?'

'His adoring secretary stepped into the breach.'

'You sound slightly bitter,' Rob observed.

'Not really. The first evening I've been asked out for ages and it was nearly ruined. It's not as if I could have postponed it, is it? You'll be off any moment and I might never see you again.'

She tried to make it sound light-hearted but realised she did mind, very much. She felt slightly shocked at the realisation. She'd been deprived of attentive male company for too long.

'Not necessarily. I might stay in the area for a while. There's quite a lot to do round these parts. You may not get rid of me that easily. Anyhow, even if I travel along for the entire day, I only ever cover a few miles. And, don't forget, the canals do twist and turn a bit, so it would usually be quite a short distance by road. I was sort of hoping we'd be able to see quite a bit of each other, actually.'

Cathy felt a glow of pleasure spreading through her and blushed. Why did she have the sort of complexion that showed up every slight blush? Blond hair may be desirable, but the fair colouring that went with it was a pain at times.

'I do believe you're blushing,' Rob said with a smile.

'I always blush. It's horrible.'

'I find it rather appealing. Well, now, have you decided which of the local hostelries you are going to take me to?' he asked.

They got into Cathy's little car, Rob having to fold his long legs in a way that looked most uncomfortable.

'Sorry, don't think this model was made for someone of your height,' she apologised.

'I'm used to folding myself into small spaces. The boat gives me plenty of practice. I've become an expert in having a shower in a five-and-a-half-foot-high bathroom.'

The evening passed all too quickly.

They laughed a lot, talked a great deal and enjoyed each other's company hugely. Cathy's main regret was that even if they did form a relationship, it probably wouldn't go on for very long. Rob was constantly moving on. He'd told her that on the first day they'd met. He was obviously unwilling to be tied to one place.

'Will you come aboard and have a coffee?' Rob offered, when they arrived back at the bridge.

Cathy hesitated. Every part of her wanted to say yes but she sensed it could be dangerous, not that she didn't trust him but she didn't trust her own feelings. It would be very foolish to allow things to get out of hand simply because she felt so attracted to him. After all, she hardly knew him and he may not share her feelings.

'I'd better not. I have an early start. I have to get Jamie's breakfast and take him to school. I don't like to let him down.'

'Good grief, doesn't his father do

anything at all for his son?' Rob burst out. 'He's really got it made, with you on call night and day. I hope he pays you well.'

'He pays me very well, thank you,' Cathy replied defensively. 'I adore Jamie and want him to be happy. The poor little soul's had to survive his whole life without a mother. David works very hard to provide for him and make sure he has a decent home.'

She was almost aggressive in defence of her boss.

'My, my, sorry. I didn't mean to touch any sore spots. Please, don't let's spoil the evening with a futile argument. I've really enjoyed it.'

'I'm sorry,' Cathy said. 'I didn't mean to snap. Believe me, I'd love to come on board for coffee but it really would make me very late home.'

'OK, forgiven, but only if you promise to come and see me again tomorrow. Bring Jamie, if you like, after school? Do you have to work weekends as well?' he added, thoughtfully.

‘Occasionally. I usually babysit in the evening if David has meetings.’

‘Only I was thinking, we could go for a longer trip, stay somewhere overnight, if you like. No, don’t look like that. I’m not suggesting anything. There’s a spare bunk in the cabin, as you must have realised. I just thought it would be fun. I can drop you back here on Sunday evening.’

‘Can I think about it?’ Cathy said breathlessly.

It sounded like paradise. A whole weekend away from her own boring life. She was about to say yes when she remembered something.

‘Blow! I promised Mum I’d go to see her and Dad for lunch on Sunday. I haven’t been over for ages.’

‘And where’s that?’ Rob asked thoughtfully.

‘Near Aylesbury.’

‘About ten miles from here?’

‘I guess, why?’

‘We could always go that way and then you could go off for your lunch. If we didn't make it all the way back here afterwards, you could always get a taxi or bus or something.'

'What, and take you to lunch with the parents? I don't think so. Mum would be choosing a hat for the wedding and Dad would be taking you on one side to find out about your prospects. They're desperate for me to settle down with a nice man.'

'Oh, and I'm not a nice man?'

'Of course you are, but, you don't want the meet-the-parents routine at this stage, surely?'

'Not really, but I'd cope. Parents usually like me. I have a way with older women. But honestly, I wasn't meaning to invite myself as well.'

His voice held a note of seriousness beneath the light-hearted tone.

'I don't know. I'll think about it and let you know tomorrow,' Cathy decided.

'Give me a call.'

He scribbled a number on a scrap of paper and passed it to her.

'Oh, I didn't realise you had a phone.

A mobile, I presume. How do you manage to charge it?'

'I have a windmill and a solar panel. They provide me with electricity for lots of things, and batteries are charged so I have lighting. All mod-cons here. I run a laptop and mobile. I suppose you don't have e-mail.'

'I'm afraid not. I know nothing about it at all, but I can phone you tomorrow. I'll ring Mum and test the waters, as it were. It all sounds lovely.'

Rob opened the car door and unwound himself from the seat. He reached over and planted a gentle kiss on her cheek.

'Thanks for a lovely evening and I shall really look forward to our weekend. Show you the joys of travelling on a narrow boat. 'Bye.'

He turned and disappeared down the path, out of sight. Cathy touched her cheek, where his lips had planted a light kiss. Her heart was beating a little faster than usual as she started her car.

A whole weekend with Rob sounded

wonderful, even if she did barely know him. It had to be instinct, she told herself. She hoped David wouldn't spring any extra demands on her. Somehow, she felt doubtful that he would manage without her, especially if he knew of her intentions.

She really wanted to take up this invitation, she realised. It was also about time she stopped thinking of David as anything more than an employer. After all, if she was beginning to harbour what might be romantic thoughts about Rob, that alone must prove something.

3

Cathy was slightly late arriving at work the next morning and immediately discovered David's mood was even worse. He was obviously suffering from a massive hangover. Though she was certainly not a prude, Cathy had never understood why people drank themselves into this state. She enjoyed a drink but couldn't bear the thought of anything approaching a hangover.

'You're late,' David accused, as he followed her into the kitchen. 'Jamie's still in bed, refusing to get up until you're here. He's getting too big for his boots. High time I thought about sending him to boarding school. You indulge him too much.'

'David, you can't be serious. He's only six years old, much too young to be away from home. He did lose his mother after all.'

She bit her tongue, wishing she had never uttered the words, but his personal jibe had found its mark and she was smarting at the implications.

'He'd be better off if I can't rely on having the help and support,' David retorted, an acid tone in his voice.

'Oh, so that's all I am, is it? Paid help. I thought I was a bit more than that.'

'You made it quite plain that's what you are, unwilling to help out with babysitting. It was a very important business meeting. I've suggested so many times that you move in here with us. There's masses of space. You'd have your own room and it would be a whole lot more convenient for all of us with you on the spot.'

'For you maybe but I'm sorry, I can't consider it. I am entitled to my own life. I work loads of hours more than I'm paid for, usually without grumbling at all.'

Cathy was angered by his unjustified complaint.

'I hadn't realised you felt so burdened. Maybe you want to put in a bill for overtime.'

She didn't return her sharp answer, seeing the stricken face of Jamie peeping round the door.

'We should talk later. I must get Jamie's breakfast or he'll be late for school,' she said gently.

Without a word, David left the kitchen and she heard him go upstairs. She heard the sound of his electric razor, followed by several doors being slammed. White-faced, Jamie sat on a stool by the breakfast bar. Silently, he spooned his favourite cereal into his mouth and drank his orange juice.

'Would you like an egg?' she asked, but he shook his head. 'Some toast?'

'No, thank you, Cathy. I'm not hungry. I'll go and brush my teeth now.'

Quite unused to this paragon of good behaviour, Cathy felt worried. Had something being going on? He came down again, dressed in his school uniform, with his bag packed.

'Have you said goodbye to Daddy?' she asked.

The boy scowled and shook his head.

'Don't you think you should?'

Jamie shook his head again and looked down sullenly.

'What's wrong, Jamie?' Cathy asked kindly.

He looked down at his feet. She put a finger under his chin and raised his face. There were tears in his eyes and his lip trembled.

'I don't want to go to boarding school,' he sobbed. 'I want to stay here, with you, for always. I wish you could be my mummy, and Rob could be my daddy.'

'James,' a voice said from the door, 'stop snivelling and go and wash your face. It's time you were leaving for school.'

Cathy watched, her heart aching as the little boy dragged himself to the cloakroom, even though his face was perfectly clean.

She turned to face an angry David.

Their eyes met and, unexpectedly, she saw pain flash across his face.

'So, things are getting serious are they, with this Rob character? How long have you known him, exactly? I hope you haven't been using my son as an excuse to spend time with him. That's not what I pay you for. I don't like it. In fact, I don't want you taking him there again. He's too young to witness whatever it is you get up to with this . . . this boatman.'

'How dare you! I have spent two short periods after school and one evening with Rob. He's a kind man who was giving a bit of his time to entertaining your son. As you must realise, any time spent with a child is usually rewarded by a bit of loyalty. Perhaps you should try it yourself sometime.'

She turned and rushed out of the kitchen, angry with herself as well as the boy's father. She shouldn't have said the things she had, even if they were true. Quickly, she gathered up

Jamie's things and took him hurriedly out to the car.

'We'll drive to school today so you won't be late.'

'Can we go and see Rob after school?' he asked, his voice still a little shaky.

'Best if we don't,' she replied. 'I'm sorry, but your daddy doesn't want you to go on the boat again.'

'Dad's mean. It's because he doesn't want me to have any fun. I hate him.'

'No, you don't, Jamie. Don't be silly. Everyone got a bit cross, that's all. Dad's very busy. He has to work very hard.'

She was always defending David, quite automatically, she realised. She took Jamie inside the gates when they arrived. He was still a tense little bundle as he left her with his usual, casual wave. She wondered what had come over David recently. He was never like this before. He seemed moody and bad-tempered most of the time recently. His behaviour was becoming quite unacceptable, but he was, after all, Jamie's father and did have the right to some control over what he did or did not allow.

She drove back to the house thoughtfully. To her surprise, David was still at home. She went into the kitchen and began to clear away the breakfast things. Most days, she spent tidying round, doing the washing and preparing an evening meal for David and Jamie. Mrs Morgan came in once a week to give the place a thorough clean. It was an arrangement that usually worked for everyone. David came into the kitchen.

'I want to speak to you again, to clear the air before I go to work.'

He sounded almost apologetic, something that was quite rare, for him.

'OK,' she replied, not willing to give anything away at this stage.

'I should have given you more notice about last night. I'm sorry. I was probably being unreasonable. It was an emergency though.'

'Apology accepted,' Cathy said with a smile, feeling relief at clearing the air. 'Usually, it wouldn't have mattered,' she said chattily, trying to explain, 'but just this once . . . '

Her relief was short-lived as David interrupted.

'I also need you to look after Jamie for a few hours tomorrow. Oh, don't worry, I'll pay you extra. Nothing taken for granted. I have to be out for a few hours during the middle of the day, say ten-thirty to four. You can help me out this time, can't you?'

Cathy's heart sank. It would completely ruin her plans but if she refused again, she might be the cause of even more grief for Jamie.

'I have got plans, actually, for the whole weekend, or what's left of it. I was going away, but I won't have Jamie upset. If it's really, really important, I could try to re-arrange things.'

'Of course it's really, really important,' he echoed sarcastically and somewhat testily, 'otherwise I wouldn't ask.'

He did look slightly guilty, Cathy thought, and wondered what exactly was so important on a Saturday. Even accountants couldn't possibly work on a Saturday.

'Were you planning more time with your boatman lover boy?' he added, snidely.

Cathy fumed. How dare he be so patronising?

'I was planning a trip on Rob's boat, yes, but if it's so vital that you go out, I suppose I'll have to forget it.'

'Thanks. Right, I'd better get to work.'

Left to herself, Cathy felt angry. She was smarting from his unpleasant comments and the look on his face actually shocked her. He looked almost vindictive and not at all the man she had admired all these years. She was still wondering exactly what David was planning to do that was so important on a Saturday. Poor Jamie. He so looked forward to the weekends spent with his dad and she had always encouraged this feeling. She also had to break the bad news to Rob. She felt in her pocket for the scrap of paper he had given to her, with his phone number. It wasn't there! She went to look in the car but it seemed to have disappeared. She'd simply have to go and see him in person.

She had already decided to take up the invitation and go with him for the weekend, but that was before David had dropped his bombshell. She had even come round to the idea of taking him to meet her parents. It was such a pity. They might even have started the trip this evening.

She glanced at her watch. She needed to do some food shopping for David and Jamie for the weekend. If she left now, she'd have time to call on Rob and do the rest of her chores before she collected Jamie. She went back to the bridge where she had left him the night before, but there was no sign of either him or his boat. She parked the car and walked a little way in one direction and then the other. It was futile. How could she have lost his number? She even went back to her flat to see if she had dropped it. Nothing. It must have blown away, she cursed herself.

By the time Jamie finished school, she was sick of looking for Rob and his phone number. Maybe if she and Jamie walked back along the canal on the way home from school, they might see him. Though David had forbidden her from taking Jamie to the boat, if they chanced to see Rob, it was by accident, wasn't it? Besides, they often walked home by that route.

Despite Jamie's excited leaping about, in case his beloved Rob was around, there was no sign of the brightly-coloured boat. It seemed that he must have moved on. Good job she hadn't called her parents yet, or they'd be getting anxious for nothing.

'Hope Dad takes me out somewhere tomorrow,' Jamie said tucking into milk and biscuits when he got home. 'He promised we'd go somewhere nice.

He's been so busy this week, he hasn't had time for anything.'

'He's a busy man, darling. He's got to go out tomorrow, I'm afraid. Sometimes he has to see clients when they have finished their own work.'

'I suppose Dad's seeing that woman, who's s'posed to be business.'

'What woman?' Cathy asked suspiciously.

'The one he saw last night. Maggie told me. She's got loads of money that Dad's sorting out for her. I s'pose that's why he wants me to go to boarding school, to get me out of the way.'

Cathy was silent. Maybe David was working, but he surely could have fitted his work into proper working hours. There must be more to it. Besides, he needed to spend time with his son. He owed it to him. Sometimes she thought he scarcely knew his own son. She knew she was being used and felt angry. How dare he treat her this way. Just so that he could spend time with some woman? If that was his plan, why hadn't he been honest about it? And why wasn't Jamie involved? If David was moving into some sort of relationship, surely his son would have to be included.

She noted with some interest that she felt not the slightest pang of jealousy at the thought of David with another woman. She must be over him, if there had ever really been anything to be over in the first place. Whatever his reasons, she did not like David being deceitful.

'Dad's home,' Jamie called a little later. 'I want to talk to him about this boarding school thing. He can't mean it, can he?'

He ran out to meet his father whom, Cathy was pleased to see, was smiling for once. He'd obviously had a better day. She hoped his temper was a little better, too.

Once she had left them to their meal, she drove down to the canal again, hoping to find Rob. She drove along the road to where another bridge crossed and got out to look along the banks for any sign of him. Nothing. It seemed he had disappeared completely. Maybe he regretted his impulsive offer and had left the area. He couldn't have gone too far, surely. He said he didn't travel very quickly at any time. She went on to the next bridge and the next and turned back and went the other way.

On the other side of the village, the canal moved right away from the road, so she parked and walked along the towpath, in the other direction. She was about to give up when she noticed a side cutting and there, moored in the quiet backwater, was Rob. He was sitting with a glass of wine in his hand, gazing down at the water.

'Cathy! You came,' he exclaimed. 'I'd given up on you. When you didn't call me, I thought I must have scared you off. I moved to a quieter spot, as you can see. Why didn't you call?'

'I'm so sorry. I lost your number. Couldn't find it anywhere. I seem to have spent half the day looking for you.'

'Does this mean you will come with me for the weekend?'

He grinned and looked so pleased that Cathy almost gave way and thought of abandoning her employer but as always, she knew she couldn't do it to Jamie. She explained what had happened and that regretfully, she had to decline the invitation. As they discussed other possibilities, a compromise was suggested. Delightedly, she agreed to meet him at four the following day and they could set out immediately towards Aylesbury. If they didn't get far enough, they could ring her parents and someone could come and collect them. Simple!

'Why not stay for supper now?' he asked. 'I've made a stew and there's plenty for two.'

'My, my, a man who cooks, almost unheard of in my family. Well, OK. I haven't any other plans. That sounds great.'

They spent the rest of the evening chatting, eating and drinking. She learned that he was a committed vegetarian and the delicious stew was made of a mixture of vegetables and pulses. She also discovered that despite his rather denigrating comments about his job as an accountant, he did a considerable amount of work right here on the boat. He used his laptop to keep in contact with his work. They realised they also shared a similar taste in music and books, giving them even more to catch up with.

'But you'll be leaving the area soon and eventually going back to wherever home is,' she said sadly.

It was pointless allowing herself to become fond of him, especially if he was about to disappear from her life. Besides, she felt a deep responsibility towards Jamie. Whatever feelings she may have thought she had for David were obviously misplaced, but Jamie was something else entirely. She loved the child as if he were her own and would never do anything to hurt him. He was also playing a big rôle in her current dilemma.

It was almost midnight before she left

the boat. Rob walked her back to her car and leaned over to kiss her, very gently, on the lips. She felt a shock of surprise. What had started as an ordinary goodbye peck on the cheek had suddenly become something so much more. She felt herself weaken and her legs turned to jelly. The surge of emotion left her breathless.

Reluctantly, she drove away from the canal back to her own flat. With a jolt, she remembered that she had forgotten to phone her parents about the changed plans for Sunday lunch. It was much too late to call them now. She'd have to wait till the morning.

Although she felt very tired, Cathy could not sleep. She tossed and turned, thinking about her future in a way she had avoided for years. She had taken her formal qualifications to be a nanny soon after she left school. She had given little thought to her long-term plans when she accepted the job with David and Jamie. Rob's probing questions during the evening had made her stop and think about herself. She needed to consider her options. She could hardly spend the rest of her life being a substitute parent for the little boy.

His father probably did intend to send him away to school eventually, but presumably not until he was much older. Besides, she was very firmly set against sending children away from their homes unless absolutely necessary. But what was she to do? She was already twenty-five and another few years with Jamie would mean that she couldn't consider having any serious relationships until she was approaching thirty. She also hoped that one day, she would have her own children, before she was too old to enjoy them, always assuming she met the right man, of course.

She sat up and put the light on. It was three o'clock. With a sense of shock, she tried to bring herself back to reality. She had only met Rob four days ago and here she was making plans for a future that would almost certainly never exist. She blushed to the roots of her hair, glad that no-one could see her or have any inkling of her thoughts. It was all just too scary. She pushed away all her silly dreams, lay down and managed to sleep.

The next morning, she phoned her parents and arranged lunch. Her mother was positively bouncing with curiosity about this man she was bringing and sounded extremely nervous at the prospect.

'Why haven't you told us about him before?' she demanded. 'Is it serious? Well, I suppose it must be if you're bringing him home to meet us. You've never done that before. Oh, dear, whatever shall I give him to eat?'

'Glad you mentioned that. He's a vegetarian.'

'Oh, Cathy,' her mother said.

'Just do your normal thing but don't roast potatoes round the meat. Rob will just eat the vegetables and certainly won't mind if we all eat meat. Don't worry about him. He's really very nice, but he's just a casual friend. One more thing, we don't know each other well enough to be serious.'

Whatever Cathy said, nothing could convince her mother that wedding bells were not in the offing.

'I've only just met him, Mum,' she protested for the umpteenth time. 'It's simply that he won't be around this area for much longer. He's invited me for a short trip in his boat and it's conveniently near you. As I'd arranged to come over anyway, it seemed rude not to invite him along. That's it, end of story. Now, please stop trying to marry us off. It isn't like that. He's just a friend.'

But it was useless. The questions went on until Cathy was inclined to tell her to forget lunch altogether.

'Let's just leave it, Mum. Forget all about lunch for this week. I'll try to come over next weekend instead.'

But the protests continued until

finally, she agreed to take Rob over the next day, after all. She felt quite exhausted and carried a deep sense of trepidation about the whole thing.

4

David was dressed casually when she arrived at their home at ten o'clock. She had packed a bag with a few necessities for the weekend and left it in the car.

'Please make sure you are back by three o'clock, three-thirty at the very latest. I mean it, David.'

'Of course,' he said amiably.

He lowered his voice then and spoke softly.

'And don't forget what I said about your boating friend. It isn't a suitable environment for a small child.'

With a few hurried instructions, he drove away, leaving her to spend the day with Jamie. The child's first request left her somewhat perplexed.

'Can we go and see Rob on his boat, please? He'll be leaving soon and I like the boat more than anything.'

'I'm sorry, Jamie, but your dad said

he didn't want you to spend time on the boat. I think you heard him say it.'

For whatever reason, she knew that David's order was quite unreasonable, but all the same, she knew she had to obey it or risk losing her job. For her own sake, it was bad enough. For Jamie it would be a disaster.

'Please, Cathy. Please let's go to Rob's boat,' Jamie begged.

'Jamie, stop it. Your father told us very clearly that he doesn't want us to visit Rob or his boat again. You understand?'

'But why? I didn't know what he meant. It's silly.'

His face looked genuinely puzzled.

'What's wrong with visiting the boat? It's so cool.'

'I know, love, but we can't do something your dad has clearly told us not to. How about us going to the park?' Cathy suggested.

'Boring,' was the response. 'Why can't we just go anyway? Dad wouldn't even know. He's the one who stopped us going out for the day, like he promised.'

Jamie had a defiant air about him that was quite out of character. Silently, she cursed the boy's father.

'Jamie, you know that would be wrong. It would be like telling lies.'

'But Dad told a lie when he said we'd go out somewhere.'

'I'm not talking about this any more.'

His logic was indisputable but he could not get away with this attitude. She tried offering other plans but everything she suggested got the same reaction. She finally gave up. Jamie mooched round, getting grumpier and grumpier. She tried to reason with him, pointing out that they'd only met Rob this week and if they hadn't, Jamie wouldn't even know about the boat.

'But I do know about it and I did go on it. I hate Dad. Can't I come and live with you, please, Cathy?'

She hugged him and tried to explain mysteries about adults that she didn't even understand herself. She sent him out into the garden while she prepared lunch.

Time moved slowly for the rest of the day. She played several games with Jamie and at last, three o'clock came. Unfortunately, David didn't. He had promised to be back as soon as he could, three at the latest. Half-past came and went; quarter to four and still no sign. At four, she became angry. Really, he was too bad.

She called Rob and promised she would be there as soon as she could. Jamie sensed her growing tension and began to play up even more. She snapped at him and he began to cry. Immediately, she felt guilty. He shouldn't have to suffer her own frustration because of his father's lack of consideration. This was probably the first time ever that she had plans when David wanted her to babysit. He took her totally for granted, that was the problem. If she didn't know better, she was almost tempted to take Jamie with her to the boat and blow any plans David might have had for the rest of the day. She contemplated using his mobile number but he rarely had it switched on and in any case, he hated being called on it.

It was after five when the telephone finally rang. She snatched the receiver and heard David's voice.

'Sorry I'm a bit late. Something's come up. I need you to stay on for the evening. I'll pay you extra, of course. I won't be back till late, so you'll need to stay over.'

'David,' she said in a voice that was deadly calm, 'I have made plans. I told you that when I gave up my Saturday for you. I am already over two hours late and I am not prepared to wait any longer. If you are not home within the next ten minutes, I shall leave and whatever your instructions were, I shall take Jamie with me.'

She put the phone down despite the fact that David was shouting into his end of the phone, wherever he was.

'Where are we going?' Jamie asked cautiously.

'Hopefully, nowhere. I expect your father will be back very soon.'

'You don't know my dad,' he said wisely, shaking his head.

He was quite right, Cathy thought. She no longer knew the man of whom she had once thought so fondly, even to the extent of imagining they might have a future together. She allowed David fifteen minutes and when he failed to show up, she went upstairs and put a pair of pyjamas and a couple of changes of clothes into a bag.

'Come on, Jamie. I know I said we couldn't go earlier but we're going on Rob's boat for a little trip.'

A look of utter delight spread over the boy's face.

'Yippee. And Cathy, you've put my jimjams in. Does that mean we're going to sleep on the boat?' he asked incredulously. 'Dad's going to go ballistic.'

For once she forgot her deep loyalty

to David, especially when dealing with Jamie.

'Too bad. If he can't spare the time to listen to what I say, he'll have to take the consequences. Come on.'

Her conscience pricked slightly at her actions. Suppose David had been farther away than her ten-minute deadline? He might have been unable to drive the distance in the time. He could always have rung again, she reasoned. But in any case, he'd been given clear warning of her intentions right from the start, when she'd reluctantly agreed to help him out.

Quickly, she wrote out Rob's mobile number and left it propped against the phone. If David managed to return, he could call to find out where they were. If he wanted to get Jamie back, he'd jolly well have to come and fetch him. They had already driven away in her car when the phone rang, back at the house, but they were quite unaware of the message left on the answering machine.

Rob was pacing the towpath when they arrived. His face was thunderous but he managed to hide his anger when he saw Jamie was with her. The little boy was so excited that he practically fell on to the boat.

'Is it OK, Rob? I mean, do you mind me coming as well?' he asked anxiously. 'And Cathy's brought my jimjams as well as other clothes. It must mean I can stay on the boat, mustn't it? To sleep,' he added, his voice rising to a high-pitched squeak in his excitement.

Rob managed a smile and said of course it didn't matter. He added that he was pleased to know that Jamie liked the boat so much. He looked questioningly at Cathy.

'David phoned to say he wasn't coming home till even later, so I thought we both deserved a bit of a treat. I'm sorry but it seemed like a good idea at the time. Maybe we should forget about the trip we planned and simply take a little cruise. We can always go back home tonight.'

'I think Jamie would like a bit longer journey, wouldn't you, young man? And he seems to want to stay overnight.'

'If you're sure,' she replied. 'But if David does phone and wants Jamie to return, we have to do what he says. Do you understand, Jamie?'

'Yeah!' he drawled. ' 'Course, but he won't, will he? He wants to stay somewhere else or he'd have come back, wouldn't he?'

'Sure,' Rob said cautiously, trying to read Cathy's expression. 'Now then, we'd better see about finding a life-jacket for you. There's wine in the fridge, Cathy. Pour us one each, will you?'

Cathy smiled in relief. It looked as if it was going to be all right, at least as far as this part of the expedition. What David would say was quite another matter. Though the threat of his anger hung over them, she was determined that they would enjoy the trip. It was a warm, early-summer evening. The settling sun lit the trees with a magical light, filtering down on to the surface of the water and sending tiny diamond sparkles in the wash behind the boat.

The countryside seemed to be decorated with flowers, pockets of colour against the greenish brown earth and grass. She pointed out different things to Jamie as they drifted along. A sudden flash of blue as a kingfisher flew by made the child shriek with joy. Rob touched her arm, smiling, sharing the pleasure of the little boy's reactions.

'You must be the worst bird-watcher ever. You'll scare it away if you yell like that,' Rob teased.

Jamie looked crestfallen for a moment but then he saw the grin and smiled himself, looking slightly sheepish.

'Sorry, Rob,' he said gently, 'but I've never seen one before, not a real kingfisher. I thought they were only in picture books.'

Rob laughed and teased him gently whenever they saw any creatures at all. Soon they were all laughing at the slightest thing, each ripple in the water and any movement they saw on the bank. They waited for the next lock, only a short distance farther on, according to the very comprehensive waterways guide. They could tell exactly where they were at most times, as everything going over the water was marked, even pipes carrying cables. Jamie was fascinated that anyone could have taken such trouble to note them.

As they approached the lock, they were all given jobs. Jamie found it hard to decide whether to stay on board the boat and watch as it rose up into the next level, or stay on the bank and watch the boat as it bobbed up to the top of the lock.

'Why do you have to have locks?' he asked. 'And why are they called locks?'

'Because water won't flow uphill and sometimes, you have to make sort of steps so that boats can go from one height to another. As to why they are called locks, I'm not sure. I expect it's to do with the water being locked at different heights. But that's only a guess.'

It was great to Cathy that he always took the trouble to answer Jamie's endless questions. David rarely seemed to be bothered.

Jamie stood in the cockpit of the narrow boat as he and Rob piloted it carefully into the narrow space. Black-looking brick walls surrounded them. The gates were shut behind them, with no room to spare between the back of the boat and the heavy wooden structures. There was a slight echo as Jamie chatted. He made a few squeaks to enjoy the sound and laughed, as Cathy groaned at winding the paddles to let the water through.

The two males both made heave-ho comments from the bottom of the lock, as she worked. At last, the trickle turned to a rush as the water broke through. Slowly, the boat rose as the water level increased and soon, Jamie was dancing about the deck as he reached the same level as Cathy.

'That was brill,' he shouted. 'I love living on a boat. It's the best, really the best.'

'I'm glad you like it so much.' Rob laughed. 'I think we need to move on now and pick up that poor, exhausted female lying on the bank over there. Has that finished you off?' he called to Cathy.

'I'm just not fit,' she admitted. 'You must have muscles the size of melons.'

'Try me sometime and find out,' Rob said suggestively.

Cathy blushed and glanced over at Jamie to see if he'd picked up on the innuendo, but he was totally lost in watching the water and the magic of his surroundings. Rob stretched his hand out and helped her back on to the boat. He held it for a few seconds and she felt a rush of affection for this unusual man. He was something very special. How many people would give up a promising career to potter round the waterways of Britain? Idealistic it may have been but she admired him for actually doing it. Most people talked about it and spent their lives dreaming of doing something like it but few actually did.

'Are we going to drive on now?' Jamie asked impatiently. 'Only I expect it will soon be bedtime and I want to see something else.'

Cathy smiled at him and touched his shoulder, feeling happier than she could remember. After a couple of hours, they moored in a quiet spot where trees overhung and meadows stretched away on either side of the water.

'I can see a trolley down there,' Jamie called as they went under a bridge. Cathy looked over the side. The water was shallower and deep in the mud was a supermarket trolley.

'There's all sorts of stuff dumped in the water. Sad that people have nothing better to do than leave rubbish everywhere. Now then, me lad, maybe I should send you down to clear the bottom. What do you say?'

Jamie looked slightly anxious until he

saw the twinkle in Rob's eye.

'Wouldn't mind, but I 'spect Cathy wouldn't let me get my clothes dirty and wet. You know what women are,' he added conspiratorially.

'Hey, watch it or I'll dump you in there myself, both of you.'

Jamie squealed in delight as she leaned towards him, pretending to try and grab him. They played all sorts of silly games, looking for things on the banks and in the water.

'Five apples for the next person to spot a lion,' Rob called.

They all laughed but Jamie won when he saw a pub alongside the water. The sign proclaimed it to be The Red Lion, where the garden was full of people, enjoying the fine evening.

'Where are my five apples?' Jamie demanded.

'You'll have to wait till I go shopping again,' Rob confessed. 'I thought I was safe to make the bet but I reckoned without your cunning genius.'

'We could always stop and have

crisps and lemonade instead,' the little cunning genius suggested.

'I'm going to moor soon and cook some supper. I think there might even be some lemonade in my wine cellar.'

Jamie found the idea of a wine cellar quite exotic but on a boat it was positively ridiculous, but Rob had a secret cupboard under the floor in the main cabin. In there he had several boxes of wine, beer and fruit juices. Both passengers were most impressed.

'Now,' he said, 'it's time we found somewhere to stay. I think there's probably somewhere just around the next bend. All hands on deck.'

The willing crew stood up and waited for him to pull into the side. He cut the engine and drifted gently to the bank, then pulled out two long, hooked spikes and a mallet and handed it to Jamie.

'Stand on the edge of the boat and once we stop, leap for the bank. You'll have to hammer the spikes hard into the ground and then we can tie the ropes to it.'

The child looked slightly worried and Cathy stood ready to help. Rob put his hand on her arm and shook his head slightly. He wanted the boy to have the responsibility himself and know that he would have to help in the end. All the same, it was good for him to try on his own.

'You're brilliant with him. I'd almost think you were a parent yourself,' she whispered.

'No such luck,' Rob replied with a grin. 'But I did have two older brothers who made me do all sorts of chores. Made me much more capable and it gave me a sense of independence, even though I usually complained bitterly at the time. Right, young man, how's it going?'

He leaped easily on to the bank and Cathy heard him praising Jamie for his efforts. The little boy was pink in the face with his exertions. Rob took the mallet and gave the spikes one more hefty swing. Jamie helped fasten the ropes and never once complained about a thing. Most unusual for him.

They sat on the deck as darkness was falling, listening to the gentle sounds of water lapping against the boat. It was so peaceful.

'Daddy ought to come on a boat,' Jamie said thoughtfully.

'What makes you say that?' Cathy asked, slightly surprised.

She knew David would hate the slow pace of life on board.

'Because he's always too busy and that makes him cross. It's slow and lazy on boats. At least, it is on this sort of boat. Then maybe he wouldn't always be tired and grumpy.'

'I think he might get a bit bored. It's probably all a bit too slow for him.'

'S'pect so. Shame though 'cos I really, really like boats.'

Cathy was surprised by his perception. All the same, she agreed that David would find the whole pace of life on a canal much too sluggish. Jamie was right — it might have done him good. Rob emerged from the galley, having produced another delicious meal and they sat out on the deck to eat it. Jamie made no complaints at eating every scrap of the vegetables he usually claimed to hate. Typical child, she thought. Put him in different surroundings and he behaved like a paragon. Long may it last!

'I suggest Jamie goes to bed in my bunk and then we can still use the cabin,' Rob suggested. 'It will get cold quite soon. We can always move him later.'

Once the little boy was safely tucked up in Rob's bunk, Cathy began to have doubts about her actions.

'David will be absolutely furious,' she said softly, biting her lip anxiously.

'Call him and explain,' Rob suggested sensibly, handing her the mobile.

She dialled David's number and got the answering machine, so she left a brief message.

'It was the third message, according to the bleeps,' she remarked. 'He still isn't home. I'm glad I didn't wait, though, come to think of it, David has probably been trying to call me. Maybe I'd better try his mobile, if that's OK.'

Rob nodded. There was no reply and again, she was invited to leave a message.

'I really don't understand,' Cathy said, shaking her head.

'Presumably, he's having a good time and decided to stay over. He's obviously given up bothering, realises that his principles are lower than his desires or something.'

He tried to speak lightly, though he could see it wasn't working. Somehow, the mood of the evening was destroyed. However much Rob tried to stop her from worrying, he was unsuccessful. He played music that he knew she liked and tried to talk about some of the things they'd both been interested in the previous night. By eleven o'clock, he was ready to give up.

'I'm sorry to spoil everything,' Cathy whispered. 'It's just so peculiar. I really thought David might have had the police out looking for us by now, but he doesn't even seem to have come home. I'll give it one more try.'

This time, there were five messages waiting, according to the number of bleeps.

'Look, we can go back in the morning but I can't use the engine in the dark. I don't have bright enough lights and it's considered very anti-social by other boat users. The wash disturbs everyone.'

'I'm sorry,' Cathy repeated.

'Stop apologising. Don't worry. I understand, but I am concerned about you. Are you planning to devote the rest of your life to someone else's child or do you intend having a future of your own?'

'Oh, Rob, don't put it that way. I adore Jamie and so far, it's never been a problem. But if David really has got himself a girlfriend, which I suspect he has, I'm out of a job anyhow.'

'I'd like to think there was at last something for us to look forward to.'

'Us?' she asked.

'Cathy, you must realise how I feel about you.'

'But we hardly know each other. I mean it's only a few days since we met.'

She felt another of her wretched blushes beginning to creep over her. Her eyes looked troubled.

'Maybe, but I know what I feel. Sometimes, the length of time itself makes no difference. You instinctively know what is right. Don't worry, I'm not trying to hurry you into anything. Given time, I'm sure we shall find we have even more in common. In fact, I think it's quite safe to say I think I'm already falling in love with you.'

He reached over and pulled her towards him. His arms encircled her and she felt wonderfully safe and sheltered. His kiss was tender.

'Oh, Rob,' was all she could whisper. 'If only . . . '

She stopped as his mouth once more covered hers. She gave in to her feelings and when they broke apart again, she spoke.

'Please, you mustn't spoil everything by rushing it. I do have my commitments to Jamie. He has been a large part of my life for so long. He was only two years old when I took the job. Oh, it's all so complicated. I . . . well . . . I don't want to let him down.'

'Maybe you should go and keep Jamie company,' Rob said suddenly. 'I'll bunk down in here. It's fine, honestly.'

He would hear no more of her protests and, wearily, she crawled into the large bunk next to Jamie. He stirred briefly in his sleep but did not wake. Thoroughly exhausted, she fell asleep quickly. The following morning, Jamie woke her excitedly. He shook her, bouncing on the bunk.

'Come on, Cathy. Rob's making breakfast, I think. I can smell something cooking. Isn't this great? It's the very best thing that ever happened to me.'

His face was wreathed in smiles and

his blue eyes shone out from the freckled face. She sat up, confused by the unfamiliar surroundings, almost bumping her head on the low overhang. She felt heavy and had a slight headache, as she remembered the events of the previous day. The scent of fresh coffee wafted through and she climbed out of the bunk, pulling on her jeans and a sweater and went to track down the source of the smells.

Before even sampling the coffee whose aroma drew her, Cathy tried once more to phone David. There were still a number of beeps, indicating unheard messages at home. It looked as if David had never returned to the house at all. Thoughts flooded through her, mainly angry ones. How could he stay away overnight without even checking that she was there, looking after his son? Maybe some of the messages were from him and she was misjudging him. It was most frustrating not to be able to access the messages without going back to the house.

'I'm really worried, Rob,' she confided, once Jamie was out on the deck. 'He may have left messages for me to say where he was. I left your number by the phone but he can't have found it. I'm beginning to think that something's seriously wrong.'

'What do you want to do, love?' Rob asked. 'It'll take at least a couple of hours to get back to your car, if we go by boat, and probably almost as long to walk.'

'When are we having breakfast?' Jamie demanded. 'I'm just about starving.'

'Let's eat first. Then we can sort out our next move,' Rob suggested.

'If you think so,' Cathy agreed, still worried.

'What's up?' Jamie asked, seeing the looks on the adults' faces.

Gently, Cathy tried to explain without alarming the child. He looked crestfallen at the thought of having to bring his adventure to an end.

'I expect Dad's just staying over to

work some more, with his girlfriend. Are you Rob's girlfriend now, Cathy?'

The two looked at each other and smiled. Inevitably, Cathy blushed. Rob stepped into the momentary embarrassing silence.

'She's certainly my friend and she's also a girl so you could say that.'

They ate scrambled eggs and toast, with a couple of fried field mushrooms Rob had spotted over the fence. They sat on the deck, enjoying the morning air. A swan paddled by lazily, looking with interest to see if there were any scraps going. Jamie stuck a hand out with a small piece of toast in it. The swan stretched its neck up and snatched the piece.

'Ouch. It bit me,' Jamie wailed.

'You should have let it go a bit sooner. You'll be all right. Now, Cathy, let's decide. What do you want to do?'

'Think perhaps I'd better call a taxi. That way, I can get back to the house and see what's going on. Can we work out exactly where we are?'

They spent the next few minutes poring over the waterways map. There was a road about a quarter of a mile away from where they were. A track was marked leading to it, just a few yards farther along the towpath. A taxi would get her home in a few minutes.

'How do I know where to get a taxi?' Cathy wailed. 'I don't exactly carry a number in my head. I never use them.'

Rob smiled, dialled a number on the mobile and seconds later was ordering a taxi.

'Mobile phones have a help line,' he muttered as he waited for the connection. 'Ten minutes? Great. Thanks. Right.'

He gave clear directions to the driver and switched off the phone.

'Let's get a move on. We have a short walk to get to the road. Come on, Jamie, life-jacket off and we'll be on our way.'

'You're coming, too?' Cathy asked, taken aback for a moment.

'Of course. I'm hardly going to

abandon you, am I? If something's wrong, you'll need some support, even if it's only to look after this young man. Now, got everything you need? I'll lock up, and then over the fields we go.'

5

Jamie trotted along beside them, almost running to keep up. He was totally bewildered, not realising how anything could be wrong. Seemingly, he hadn't missed his father at all. As long as Rob was included in the party, he was happy to leave the boat, feeling reassured that they would eventually have to return there.

The taxi was moving slowly along the road, obviously looking for them, as they emerged from the track. He stopped and backed to pick them up. Cathy gave him the address and what seemed like only moments later, they pulled up outside Jamie's home. It looked exactly as they'd left it the previous evening, no curtains drawn, no car outside. It was all very odd.

'Look, I was thinking. We might need your car. Why don't we get the taxi to drop me off down by the canal, where you left it and I'll drive it back here?' Rob suggested.

Cathy nodded, handing over her car keys. She let herself into the house, calling David's name loudly. It was just possible that he could have got a taxi home and gone straight to bed when he got in and never even missed them. Jamie clutched her hand, as if sensing her mood of foreboding.

The house remained silent. She saw the phone lights flashing and pressed the play button. As she heard the first message, her heart sank. It was from the local hospital, the accident and emergency department. David had been involved in a car accident! She felt sick. The second and third gave equally bleak messages, nothing more than an urgent request for her to contact the hospital. The next message was her own call and she switched off the machine. Jamie tugged at her hand.

'What does it mean, Cathy?' he whispered, his face white.

'Daddy's had an accident in his car. Look, I'd better phone the hospital. How about you going upstairs and . . . and clean your teeth,' she said.

Anything to get him away, she decided, while she tried to discover exactly what had happened.

'Then you can go and stand outside to wait for Rob. OK? He might not know which house it is. The taxi went away quite quickly. It really would help if you were out there.'

Jamie nodded, still looking extremely worried.

'Can I wait and see what's happened?'

'I'll call you as soon as I hear anything. Go on, Jamie, please.'

Her heart thudding with her anxiety, she re-played the message and wrote down the number of the hospital. When she got through, the ward sister was helpful though remained very non-committal, once she knew Cathy was not a relative. Quickly, Cathy explained the situation and managed to gain a little more information.

It seemed that David had been involved in a head-on collision with another car and had to be cut out of his badly-damaged car. Both his legs were broken and there appeared to be some concern about his future prognosis. At this stage it was impossible to tell how much lasting damage had been caused. Apart from all that, he was suffering from severe shock and trauma. At the moment they believed there was no further, more serious damage. Inevitably, they were awaiting the results of a number of tests.

'May we come and see him?' she asked in a whisper.

'You can, of course, but his son won't be allowed into the ward yet. Six years old, you say? He's too young at this stage to cope with the sight of all the apparatus round his father. I'm sorry, but it's for his own good. I expect that presents a few problems, does it?'

'I can sort something. I'll be over in a short while.'

She put the phone down and realised she had tears rolling down her cheeks. She saw that Jamie was sitting on the stairs, watching and waiting for her to speak. He looked so afraid she went over and sat down beside him.

'Is he died?' Jamie asked blankly.

'Dead,' she corrected automatically. 'No, Jamie, he isn't dead, but he's hurt his legs quite badly. He has to stay in hospital for a bit. Probably quite a long while, actually.'

'Will I see him?'

'Not until he's a bit better. He still has some machines around him, helping to make sure he is getting better. He had a very bad car crash on his way home, yesterday.'

Suddenly, Cathy felt cold, as realisation dawned. He must have been on his way home to them, yesterday afternoon. Because she had threatened to take Jamie with her, he must have been hurrying and not taking proper care. It was all her fault. Hugging Jamie, she rested her chin on his head. She had to do everything she could for Jamie. His little body began to shake as he allowed himself to cry. After several minutes, he looked up at her.

'What's going to happen to me? Who's going to look after me?'

'I am of course, darling. Don't worry about that, not for one minute. I shall be here for you, all the time. I promise.'

Jamie made no response and Cathy could see there was something still bothering him, apart from the news about his father. She asked what was wrong.

'But what about Rob? Aren't you going to live on his boat with him?'

'Of course not,' she said in surprise. 'Whatever gave you that idea?'

'You like him and he likes you, and the boat is the coolest thing ever. Anyone would want to go and live there all the time, if they could.'

'It takes more than wanting to live on a boat,' she muttered, considering the idea for a moment.

She sensed that for Rob, she might

even be prepared to put up with the undoubted inconveniences of life on a boat. She was spared further thoughts or questions as she heard Rob draw up in her car. They opened the door and waited as he got out. Quickly, she brought him up to date with the situation. She had to go to the hospital as soon as she could and would be grateful for Rob's help in looking after Jamie. He nodded agreement, his mind working on the possibilities.

'Seems there are several options. I can stay here with Jamie or we could both go and bring the boat back to the bridge, nearer here, or, we could come to the hospital with you and wait while you visit David. Which do you think is best?'

'Go and get the boat,' Jamie called out predictably.

'I'm not sure. Maybe Jamie's right. It would be good to have you near. At least you'll have your own base to stay in. You could stay here, of course, but that wouldn't be so good for you or perhaps, a very suitable arrangement when David comes home again. Once I've visited the hospital, I'll know a bit more, longer term. Are you really sure you don't mind taking Jamie back?'

'Yippee,' Jamie shouted, his father completely forgotten in his excitement.

Rob shook his head. Of course it wasn't a problem, he told her and obviously, Jamie would enjoy it.

'OK. I'll drop you off at the end of the track where we got the taxi. I can then drive on to the hospital. I'll come and find you later. I expect you'll be back at our bridge by then. I'll have to get a few things from my flat and bring them here. Obviously, I'll have to move here for a while, at least.'

Rob put his arms round her and drew her close. He was a very comforting, solid presence. He dropped a kiss on the top of her head and then held her away from him so he could look at her properly.

'Come on now. Don't worry. I'll help you all I can. I'm here for you.'

'Oh, Rob, I'm so sorry to land all this on you. You'll curse the day you ever invited us on board for that coffee. It's all my fault, too. If I hadn't been so selfish, demanding that David came back immediately, it might never have happened.'

'Cathy, don't be so silly. I won't hear a word of it. You can't possibly blame yourself. He was the selfish one, not returning when he said he would. In fact, expecting you to drop all your plans in the first place ranks as pretty selfish in my book.'

'I just feel so dreadful, us sitting there enjoying ourselves while he was going through all that.'

She shivered as she thought of him lying trapped in his car and then being cut out and taken to hospital.

'Right, let's get to it,' Rob ordered.

Quickly, he marshalled them out to the car and soon they were back at the little track that led to the boat.

Gosh, I didn't even give Rob the money to pay the taxi, Cathy thought as she drove away.

The hospital was in the nearby town of Milton Keynes. David had been taken straight there, once the paramedics had seen the seriousness of his injuries. She found him, head on a white pillow, looking pale and very bruised. He had one eye almost closed, angry-looking purple staining the whole area. His bed was surrounded by a huge array of bleeping, flashing equipment. She felt weak at the knees as she looked at it, glad of the advice not to bring Jamie. He would have been quite terrified, she knew. Even she was finding it hard to cope with.

'David, I'm so sorry. How are you feeling?'

Her voice shook slightly as she forced out the words.

'How do you think I'm feeling? Like death would have been an option, if you must know. Where's Jamie?' David croaked, trying to look past her.

'They wouldn't let me bring him here, not yet. He's with Rob, my friend from the boat. Don't worry, he's being very well looked after.'

'Oh, I see, and where were you? I got them to ring several times but they said there was no reply.'

His voice, though shaky, conveyed his anxiety and a degree of anger.

'Even late at night, you weren't there.'

'I told you I had plans for the weekend and well, I simply took Jamie with me. I said I would, if you didn't come home. It was all I could think of at the time.'

'I told you I didn't want my son going on that boat,' he whispered crossly, his eyes flashing angrily. 'How dare you go against my wishes!'

'Because you had let me down so badly. I'd already given up practically a whole day for you to do whatever it was that was so important.'

'If I can no longer trust you to follow my instructions . . . '

'David, this is not the time or place for this. Besides, other people were involved, too. I was supposed to be having lunch with my parents.'

She stopped. Her parents! She glanced at her watch and saw that it was already after noon. She and Rob were due at her parents at this very moment.

'Oh, good grief. David, I must make a call. I'd forgotten to tell my parents we won't be going after all. We should be there by now. They'll be expecting us at any time.'

'We? You mean he was going as well?' David asked, looking startled. 'It must be serious if he's going to meet them.'

Suddenly, his eyes closed and he lay back, exhausted. Cathy closed her eyes. This was turning into her worst nightmare. Unsure if it was all right to leave him, she touched his hand and muttered that she wouldn't be long. She went to find a phone, to break the news to her parents. They would be furious but it couldn't be helped. The circumstances were quite exceptional.

'You poor dear,' her mother said

understandingly. ‘Come over this evening instead. We can always have the roast cold. Your father and I were so looking forward to meeting your young man.’

‘I’m sorry, Mum, but everything’s up in the air. I simply don’t know what’s going to happen. In any case, I’m going to have to stay at David’s house for the foreseeable future. I’ll call you when I know a bit more. Sorry, but we’ll just have to forget about today. I’m really sorry. Speak to you soon.’

She returned to the ward, stopping to speak to the sister before she went back to David’s bedside. She explained her relationship to David and said that she had almost sole care of David’s son. There were no other relatives that she knew of. She was then given the information she wanted, as far as it was possible. They had operated on his legs and then set them in plaster, but it was not yet clear whether he would be able to walk again. Cathy went white. Not to walk again? It was such a tragedy for a man like David, only in his early thirties. She felt near to tears, confused and wondering how she would ever cope with the sort of future that was beginning to present itself.

'Oh, dear,' she said to the sympathetic nurse. 'If only I hadn't delivered my ultimatum. You see, I threatened him that if he didn't come home . . . oh, well, I'm sure you don't want to hear all this. But if I hadn't said what I did, he might not have been driving recklessly. It's all my fault.'

'I don't see why you should be thinking that way at all. I don't know much about it. Look, I'm not sure if I really should be saying this, but I'm going to tell you something, not that it will help you much, but he was well over the alcohol limit. It could possibly have serious implications. He's obviously been drinking heavily, for some time, we think. I'm talking long-term, you understand, not only this particular incident. He did give consent for a blood test at the scene. Poor man didn't really know what he was saying, but that's beside the point. He was well over the limit yesterday. In fact, the doctors have taken some further samples and, well, they think he may even have some liver damage.'

Cathy's eyes widened.

'I knew he'd been drinking rather more than usual lately, but I didn't know it was so much more. Maybe he had some problem at work. There was also some talk of a woman he'd been seeing. I'll see what I can find out. What a mess! Thanks for telling me all this. I won't say anything to anyone, of course.'

She went back to David's bedside.

'Is there anything you need?' she asked him. 'Do you want me to contact anyone from work for you?'

A look of anguish passed over his handsome features.

'This will be the final straw. I doubt I've got much future with that particular office. But, yes, you'd better break the news to them. Say I'll be in touch as soon as I can. Oh, and I could do with the charger for my mobile, and my laptop might be useful. Then at least I can keep in touch. I'm not sure where that is now. It was in the back of the car before the accident.'

'I'm sorry, sir, no mobile telephones in here. In fact, you can take his phone with you, Miss . . . er . . . '

A nurse had come into the side ward and began adjusting and checking the apparatus.

'Just call me Cathy. I'll take the phone. It might prove useful, who knows?'

'Now, I think Mr Hargreaves needs to rest. You could bring him some pyjamas and toilet things. I expect he'll be glad to get out of that hospital gown, but he mustn't have anything associated with work or anything that might cause him anxiety.'

'Right,' Cathy agreed. 'I'll be back later. Don't worry about anything, David. I'll look after Jamie. I shall stay at your place for a while, of course.'

David nodded helplessly. Whatever

was going on in his mind, he could do nothing.

'Cathy, I don't want that . . . '

He paused. She knew what he was going to say but she didn't want to hear it.

'Trust me, David, the way you always have. I love Jamie and would never allow anything to harm him in any way. I can promise you that.'

She left him lying helplessly in his hospital bed. Whatever he was thinking she could only do her best and if that included Rob's help, then so be it.

By the time Cathy got back to her flat, she realised she was starving. She hadn't had so much as a cup of coffee since breakfast and that was hours ago. She grabbed an apple and munched hungrily. She should have been tucking into roast beef or something equally delicious, at her parents' house. She frowned as she realised that little gathering would probably never happen now. After all this drama, undoubtedly Rob would want to be on his way as fast as possible. She sighed and stuffed the perishable things from the fridge into a box and packed several outfits for the coming days.

It was well into the afternoon before Rob phoned to say they were back in position near the bridge.

'How are things?' he asked cautiously.

'Not good. It's going to be quite fraught for the next few days, weeks even.'

She had no idea how prophetic her words were going to be and went on to tell him of the extent of David's injuries, omitting the part about his possible alcohol problems.

'But how did it happen? Was anyone else involved and if so, how are they?'

'The other car was evidently deflected off the road and landed in a load of brambles. Lucky for him, it was a soft landing. He had cuts and bruises but nothing serious. It seems David had been drinking, Rob. Please don't mention that to Jamie. Poor kid's confused enough as it is.'

She then drove to the bridge to see them both. Jamie was happily looking through piles of maps and greeted her casually.

'Oh, hi, Cathy. We've had such a good time. I steered the boat into the lock coming back and Rob let me stay on the boat by myself right through the lock. And did you know, Rob has a windmill on the boat? That's the long pole thing. I asked if it was dead but Rob said it was only asleep. I didn't know you get a sleeping windmill, did you?'

She stared at him, thinking that he seemed not to have realised anything was amiss. He caught her gaze.

'Oh, I forgot. Is Dad all right?'

'He's rather poorly, as a matter of fact. He's going to stay in hospital, as we said before.'

'Oh, good. Does that mean I can stay on the boat with Rob? Good job the holidays are coming. I can easily miss the rest of term. Nobody will mind.'

'You most certainly can't, young man, and in any case, I imagine Rob will want to get on with his trip. You have school for another two or three weeks at least. It won't be easy but we'll manage it all somehow.'

'I wouldn't dream of leaving you when you need help,' Rob insisted. 'I've got a degree in babysitting, so no worries.'

Cathy giggled as her tension was lightening. Rob seemed to have the most comforting way with him.

'Have you really got a degree?' Jamie asked.

'Certainly have.'

'But not in babysitting? Anyway, I'm not a baby any more. Dad said so.'

They arranged that Rob would take Jamie home and put him to bed, while she was visiting the hospital. Rob would stay until she got back and then return to the boat. They would make the rest of the arrangements once they could have some idea of how the future looked.

David was still in an unreasonable, grumpy mood when she arrived at the hospital and snapped at her during much of the visit. She ventured to ask if there was anyone he wanted her to call, hoping he would mention the mysterious woman friend or client that Jamie had mentioned, but no. He told her to look for Maggie's number in his phone book and call her at home. That way she would be able to let everyone at work know about the accident. When she finally took her leave of David to return home, she felt totally drained and quite exhausted. As she parked outside the garage, Rob came to the door.

'You look whacked,' he said, drawing her into his arms. 'Come and sit yourself down. I've made some soup. Decided you would probably refuse to eat anything more than that and I didn't want you fading away.'

'You're a star,' she said as lightly as she could manage. 'Soup is just right. Not sure what you could find to put in it, however.'

It felt wonderfully cosy sitting on the comfortable sofa next to him, eating his delicious concoction of vegetable soup.

'This is amazing,' she told him.

'Just a few bits and pieces I found in the fridge. Hope you didn't mind me rummaging?'

She shook her head and lay back, closing her eyes. It already seemed years since they were happily pottering along the canal enjoying the birds and flowers.

'Jamie all right?' she asked, for the first time since her return.

Rob smiled and nodded. He regaled her with tales of bathtime and how Jamie had tried to con Rob into letting him stay up till at least ten o'clock, as he claimed he always did.

'I suppose I'd better go now,' he said, his expression almost questioning his actual words.

'I guess so. Sorry, it's rather a long walk at this time of night, though. Maybe you could sleep on the sofa, if you wanted to. It's quite comfortable.

But perhaps you'd rather get back.'

She suddenly remembered she hadn't called Maggie and excused herself. She left him to think about her offer and she delved into the desk and found the number. Maggie was predictably shocked as well as sounding irritated that she was only being told this late at night. Cathy explained that she had only just got back.

'How on earth will you manage with hospital visits and looking after the poor, dear, little boy? He must be devastated, his father being so ill.'

Cathy refrained from saying that the poor, dear, little boy was happier than he'd been in ages, having his beloved Rob to look after him! She managed to persuade Maggie that she really could manage and that she didn't need her to rush round immediately or even the next morning. Tactfully, she omitted all mention of Rob, knowing it would not go down well. When she finally got away, Rob was already carrying down spare blankets from the airing cupboard.

'I decided you were right. It is too far to walk back tonight and I expect you'll need the car first thing for Jamie's school run.'

Cathy bit her lip slightly. She was regretting her slightly impulsive offer. David would go absolutely crazy. All the same, she and Rob both knew it was the sensible thing for him to stay and as it was all perfectly innocent, who could justify any complaints?

Jamie was still in a state of high excitement the following morning, especially when he discovered Rob was asleep on the sofa.

'Do I have to go to school?' he pleaded.

'Of course, you do,' Cathy told him. 'And very soon, so hurry up. I'll drive you instead of walking as we're already rather late.'

'But I should go and see Daddy, shouldn't I?'

'Good try, mate,' Rob said as he walked into the kitchen. 'Sorry, I should have made coffee and breakfast.'

'No, you shouldn't. Cathy always

does it, don't you?' Jamie chatted happily. 'But it's a shame to miss a day with Rob. We could go out on the boat and all sorts of things. I could learn much more than if I go to school.'

'I'll see you this evening,' Rob assured him. 'If we can organise it, maybe I'll take you for a trip in the holidays, if your dad agrees, of course.'

'Fat chance of that. I think he's jealous of you and he won't let us even go on the boat, will he, Cathy?'

'Come on now. We'll have to see what happens. Get your teeth brushed and we'll be off.'

'Can you drop me at the boat, on the way?' Rob asked

Cathy felt surprisingly disappointed. She realised she had been hoping to spend some time with Rob on her own but she didn't want to force anything. He'd been more than kind already and he must have things to do for himself.

' 'Course I will. What are your plans?'

He had some work to do, he told her, for a client he still had. It would take most of the morning, he thought, but he would see them both when Jamie finished school. He would look after Jamie while she went to the hospital. Obviously, he didn't want to spend much time with her after all, she decided ruefully.

Left on her own, back at the house, Cathy felt a sense of anti-climax. She was also feeling confused in her mind. Before she had met Rob, she had no real sense of urgency about the future. Though the subject of boarding school had come up recently, she had not considered it was a serious suggestion, or even a threat because she had done something David did not approve of. She needed to face up the fact that her time with Jamie was limited. She was also very attracted to Rob but that itself might be something of a fantasy. He seemed keen enough to spend time with her but he wasn't exactly asking to carry her off into the sunset.

'I hate uncertainty of any sort,' she muttered to herself.

6

Cathy phoned the hospital during the morning. David had spent a fairly comfortable night, but was feeling frustrated and angry. A visit might be beneficial, she was told. She arranged to go in soon after lunch, knowing it would limit the time she spent there, as she needed to be back for Jamie.

In some ways, she was glad to have that excuse. David was never at his most charming when he was frustrated, as she well knew. She hesitated, wondering if she might call Rob to let him know her movements but decided against it, in case it interrupted his work. It seemed strange to think of him doing someone's accounts, sitting on a boat!

David was indeed extremely grumpy and she felt she could hardly wait to get away. He gave her a long list of instructions for his office and tried to organise how she should occupy herself for the next few days at home.

'David,' she said calmly, after he had snapped out his orders, 'please be quiet!'

It was almost worth being rude, just to see his expression.

'I am living in your house while you are here and consequently, I am officially on duty for twenty-four hours a day. Now, I think it's up to me how I organise everything. I am pleased to be able to do it for Jamie's sake but I will not be dictated to in this way. I may need to have help from other people and whom I choose to give that help is up to me.'

'Maggie will help. I know she will,' he insisted.

'Fine. I'll call on her when and if I need to, but I am entitled to see whom I want to see, and there's nothing you can do to stop me.'

He muttered on for some time about the unsuitability of someone who lives on a barge, as he insisted on calling it, as company for his precious son. Cathy bit back her tongue, refusing to be baited and antagonise him any further.

'Right, well, if there's nothing else, I should get back to collect your son from school. I'll pass your messages on to Maggie and no doubt, she will be in to see you soon. I'll pass on your love to Jamie, shall I? 'Bye, David. I hope you feel better soon.'

He was still blustering as she walked out of the ward. She smiled sympathetically to the nurses, glad she didn't have to cope with him for the present. She glanced at her watch. There was just time to get home and call Maggie before she went to fetch Jamie from school.

There were several messages waiting on the answering machine, various colleagues from work and three from Maggie herself. There was also one from Rob, suggesting she stopped off at the boat with Jamie on her way home. She was pleased to hear from him but felt it might have been even better if he'd wanted to see just her. She felt cross with herself for the slight resentment. How could she be jealous of a six-year-old child?

Maggie offered to visit the hospital for the evening session and Cathy accepted gratefully. It would mean he could pass on his work-associated messages directly and also leave her free to relax with Jamie and, possibly, Rob. She walked to school to collect Jamie and then back to the boat. He chatted happily the entire journey, barely asking about his father's state of health but much more interested in what they and Rob might do for the evening.

'I wrote all about the weekend in my diary at school. Miss Higgins said it was very good.'

'Did you tell her about Daddy, too?' she asked.

'Oh, I forgot. Sorry, I'll tell her tomorrow,' he promised.

The significance of his priority was

not lost on his nanny.

As the weather was slightly cool and threatening rain, they decided to walk back home and have a meal there, rather than stay on the boat, much to Jamie's disgust. He was mollified by the fact that Rob was also coming back with them.

'Can we play Ludo after tea?' he asked.

'As long as you don't cheat,' Rob agreed.

After an hour's play, Jamie was packed off to bed and Rob and Cathy were at last alone. She felt slightly nervous, unsure of what to expect. She told him about the visit to David and how he had tried to prevent their meeting.

'I hope you told him what to do,' he spluttered, furious at the implications.

'Sort of,' she replied, 'but it's difficult. I don't want him threatening to send Jamie away again. He's too small to go away to school. He's still only six, for goodness' sake.'

'He doesn't deserve to have a child. What happened to his wife?'

'He says very little. I suppose it's too painful for him to remember. I gather she died when Jamie was born and he is still very angry about her death. She was something very special and I suppose he holds some sort of resentment that he was left with a baby instead of his beloved wife. It's very hard for him.'

'All the same, he shouldn't take out his resentment on his son. Good job he's got you.'

'Which is partly why I don't want to rock any boats, no pun intended.'

'I understand, really, I do. But you have to think of yourself, if only just a little.'

'I know, I do. But there's never been any need before. I had no reason to make any long-term plans.'

'Before what?' he pried and she coloured, looking away. 'Before you met me?'

'I suppose that's what made me stop

and take stock, if you like.'

'That sounds very promising,' he whispered, putting his arm round her shoulders.

He leaned forward and kissed her tenderly on the lips. She felt herself drawn to him in a way she had never experienced with anyone else. He was not at all like any man she had ever met before. He was unconventional, caring, funny, lovely. She blushed again at her thoughts.

'Tell me?' he insisted. 'Come on, tell me. What are you thinking?'

'I haven't met anyone quite like you before.'

'I know. I'm unique, as you are, my dear Cathy.'

His arms around her felt wonderfully comforting. When he kissed her again, she felt as if she was soaring above the earth. It all felt so right.

'So, when are we going to meet your parents?' he asked suddenly.

'My parents?' she echoed.

'I was going to meet them yesterday

but it sort of got cancelled, if you remember.'

'Was it really only yesterday? I feel as if a century has passed since then. But, in answer to your question, I don't know. Isn't it being a bit serious to take you home to see my parents?'

'Maybe, but I think I am pretty serious. After all, I have altered my plans to be here with you. That must prove something.'

His eyes were crinkling at the corners again as he tried to stifle a grin.

'You shouldn't tease,' she objected. 'I'm never sure when you're being serious.'

'One of your most endearing qualities, my love.'

She felt a thrill at his words. Was she really his love? Just a phrase, of course.

'We'd better not fix anything just yet. I'm simply not sure what's going to happen over the next few days, but I promise, you will meet them as soon as it's practical, once we know what will happen to David. Don't forget the poor guy's stuck in plaster with the threat that he may never walk again and with drink-driving charges hanging over him. What's that going to do to his future and his career?'

'As long as you promise you are really going to give some thought to your long-term future, I'll settle with that for now.'

'And what about you?' she asked. 'Have you made any long-term plans? You can't drift about on a narrow boat for the rest of your life.'

'I suppose not, but I have my qualifications. People always want good accountants.'

They chatted about the courses their lives had taken. Rob hated the thought of being an accountant for the rest of his life. He wanted adventure and excitement instead of a dull office job. This was what had driven him to follow his current plan.

'Ideally, I'd like a pretty, caring, lovely lady to join me as my crew. The position's vacant. How about applying?'

She laughed and pushed him away.

'I'm not even going to answer that and you well know why. Now, I'm going to make some coffee. Interested?'

'If that's the best you can offer, what choice do I have? Seriously, Cathy, give it some thought. You'd love living on my boat, I just know it.'

'Maybe, but I don't exactly see how I'd earn a living, do you? And there's my flat to consider.'

'You only rent your flat, don't you? That would be a huge saving, if you gave that up.'

'It still leaves the question of Jamie. I can't simply walk away, especially not at the present time.'

'I'm not asking you to. Of course I realise that's impossible. But think about it. In a few weeks, maybe something will get sorted out. David will have to sort himself out, at the very least.'

'We couldn't have organised worse timing to meet, if we'd tried, could we?' she said unhappily. 'Now, is it to be the sofa again or are you going back to the boat?'

She tried to sound businesslike about it but it was not easy.

'I suppose I'd better go back to the boat. Your reputation will be shot with the neighbours if I go on staying here.'

He looked out of the window.

'Second thoughts. It's pouring down with rain, absolutely pelting down. I think I'd better stay, if you don't mind.'

'Fine. You're welcome to the sofa.'

The next few days took on a similar pattern. Rob proved a tower of strength, babysitting while she visited the hospital. He often cooked while she was away and they shared their meals when Jamie was in bed. Jamie had accepted his presence without question and it was an enjoyable, easy routine. When left on their own, they were aware of their growing relationship and each of them began to consider the other as an important part of each other's life. Cathy was reticent about saying too much, knowing that everything could change when David returned home.

The first weekend after the accident, Jamie begged to go and stay on the boat. He said it didn't even matter if they made a trip or not, he simply wanted to be on board.

'I want to have a proper shower and sleep there again,' he said firmly.

The idea of a shower on a boat still seemed slightly exotic and infinitely preferable to any number of hot baths in his own home.

'What do you think?' Rob asked. 'We could take your car and park it somewhere, so you could go to the hospital and I can move on a bit and wait for you to come back.'

'Maybe we could go in the morning,' Cathy suggested. 'I must go and see David now and it would be a bit late when I get back.'

That simply wasn't good enough for Jamie and he pleaded with them to go right away.

'You can come back to us on the boat. Rob can put me to bed on the boat. I promise I'll be extra good. Please, please, please, Cathy.'

'Oh, all right,' she finally agreed.

Jamie was delighted and they quickly packed a few things to take.

'I'll drop you off on my way. This is becoming something of a habit.'

When she arrived at the hospital, she found David was beginning to make progress. He'd been taken off the various monitors for a couple of days and he was beginning to get restless.

'They want to start physiotherapy next week. I might be able to walk again, after all,' he said with a grimace.

'That's wonderful,' Cathy said enthusiastically. 'You're certainly looking better already. You must have been so worried. Well, we all were.'

'When's Jamie coming to see me? I'd like you to bring him tomorrow afternoon, if they permit it. What do you think?'

Though she had been expecting the request, she realised that Jamie would hate missing even a moment of his time on Rob's boat.

'What's the matter?' David asked seeing her expression.

'Nothing. Of course I'll bring him over tomorrow. I'm sure he's longing to see you.'

'Where is he now?'

'I left him with Rob. He's perfectly all right, don't worry. I wouldn't have left him if I didn't think Rob was capable of taking care of him.'

'Just as long as you don't let him go anywhere near that damned boat you were talking about.'

Immediately, Cathy's face went a fiery red.

'You haven't let him go on the boat, have you? I expressly forbade it. How dare you go against my wishes? You're not fit to have charge of a child. I insist you get him back home where he belongs, right away.'

'But he'll be devastated if you make

me take him home. He'll resent you even more.'

'How dare you! If I wasn't stuck here in this bed, I'd drive him home myself.'

David's voice was raised and a nurse came rushing in to see what was happening.

'Now, Mr Hargreaves, you must calm down. This is no good for you at all. What's the problem? Anything I can help with?'

'This stupid girl's allowed my son to go on some canal barge, when I forbade it completely.'

'I expect your boy would enjoy that,' the nurse said, grinning at Cathy. 'Help him to get through the shock of his father's injuries, I wouldn't be surprised.'

'But some idiot of a man is looking after him. He isn't competent or anything. I don't even know him.'

David was almost unable to get his words out, he was so furious.

'Well, if you don't know him, I'm sure you can't say he is incompetent.

I'm sure Cathy here would never leave him with anyone unsuitable.'

'He just happens to be her latest boyfriend. Very convenient for them, my being stuck here.'

'Now, Mr Hargreaves, I must insist on calm. I shall have to ask Cathy to leave if you can't be quiet. And you should just take time to think about the reason for you being stuck in here.'

'I think I should leave now anyway. I'm so sorry, David,' Cathy said awkwardly. 'You have to allow me to judge my own actions for the time being. I do know what is best for Jamie, and Rob has been kindness itself. He plays with Jamie and talks to him in a way that makes the boy feel happy and secure. If it hadn't been for Rob, I don't know how I would have coped this last week. And as for Jamie, he would have been terribly upset about you had Rob not helped to look after him. I'll bring him in tomorrow, if the nurse says it's all right.'

She got up to leave as the nurse nodded to her.

'It might do him good to see his son. I'm sure it will be fine tomorrow afternoon, if you can manage it.'

Cathy hoped she would be able to manage it, without causing too much of a row with Jamie. She just knew it would be difficult to tear him away but she really must allow his father to see him. It was only fair.

As expected, Jamie did rebel against any visit when she told him.

'But I can go and see Daddy one night after school,' he protested. 'Then I won't miss any time on the boat.'

'But it's ages since you saw your daddy. He's missing you.'

Nothing she could say made Jamie keen to see his father and she began to despair of ever making the wretched visit. She finally told the little boy that he would never go on the boat again, if he continued to make such a fuss. It was especially difficult, as she fully understood his reasons for not wanting to go. She certainly couldn't blame him. David was most often too busy to spend time with his son and often bad-tempered. She had always made excuses for him before but now realised that there was a much deeper problem, the reason for which was not entirely clear.

'Tell you what,' the ever-resourceful Rob intervened. 'If you go to see Dad, I'll have a special treat ready for supper, on the boat, of course.'

'What sort of treat?' Jamie asked suspiciously.

'Have you ever eaten vegetables roasted on a genuine Moroccan stove?'

The child's eyes widened and he shook his head. He didn't much like vegetables but if they were what Rob ate, he would go along with it. Minutes later, the agreement was reached. They were to go the following afternoon, as suggested. Cathy felt yet another surge of gratitude towards this unusual man. The rest of the evening was spent lazily, listening to music, eating and drinking and revelling in the peace.

The hospital visit went reasonably well. Jamie was full of the wonderful boat and Cathy felt desperately uncomfortable the more he chatted. David said little but she could see his anger simmering beneath the surface. At least he kept it to himself for the child's sake. Jamie prodded the plasters on his father's legs and even wrote his name on each of them. He was amused at the idea and only slightly curious about the outcome. He asked what would happen if he pulled on the traction cables and was told speedily and firmly not even to think of it! He stared at the fading bruises on David's face, acknowledging that it must have hurt quite a lot.

Once he had finished his exploration of the ward, he was anxious to leave and began to shuffle around. Once more Cathy realised how little they actually knew each other. She had never spent much time with the two of them together, always leaving them after her day's work finished.

'Can we go now?' Jamie begged, after half an hour had passed.

'Come on, son,' David said rather pompously. 'I haven't seen you for ages. Tell me about school, and what you've been doing.'

'Not much to say. The best bit's been going on Rob's boat. It's six feet ten wide and seventy feet long. I don't know how much that is in metres 'cos that's what Rob says, in feet and inches, not like we do at school. It's quite big, isn't it? And there's a shower and everything. The kitchen's ace. Even Cathy thinks so. Oh, there is a fridge as well.'

He prattled on, warming to his subject. He described the red and green paintings and the traditional roses and castle designs on the door. David listened, his lips pursed in disapproval.

'And what about safety?' he demanded. 'You don't swim very well.'

'I'm never allowed outside the cabin without a life-jacket and if I walk along the sides, I have a sort of dog lead thing in case I fall in. I wouldn't though. Fall in, I mean. It's too dirty.'

Cathy smiled at his descriptions but felt secretly pleased that the little boy was so aware of the safety restrictions. That must surely make his father less anxious.

'You'd better get back to it, then,' David said suddenly. 'I'd just like a word with Cathy before you go. Come and see me again soon.'

He reached out to grasp the child in a hug. Jamie looked slightly surprised. His father was not usually demonstrative as he considered it wasn't manly to give hugs. Uncomfortably, he tried to hug him back but it was difficult because of the high hospital bed. Cathy nodded to him as he began to walk uncertainly towards the door.

'I'll catch you up,' she told him. 'Now, David, what did you want to say?'

'I'm not at all happy about this boat business. The boy's obsessed with it. I realise there's nothing I can do about it from here but I want it to stop. I don't want him going near that foul, stinking water. It isn't safe. Once this weekend is over, you're to keep him at home. Take him out somewhere if you like, but not on the canal.'

He spat out the words with such feeling that Cathy was astounded. There was something more to it than mere jealousy.

'Let's wait to see what is going to happen to you,' she said, trying not to commit herself to make a promise she neither wanted to keep nor felt to be reasonable.

'They're talking about sending me to Oxford for rehabilitation or something.'

'That could make visiting difficult,' she told him.

'Since when was anything easy?' he replied sourly.

7

David did in fact begin a series of intense physiotherapy sessions. They had now decided to keep him in the local hospital, which eased the growing pressure on Cathy. She was planning to make her regular hospital visits the following weekend, trying to fit it in with the scheme to take the boat somewhere new, when the phone rang.

It was David. She was somewhat surprised when he told her it was inconvenient for her to take Jamie in the following day and would she please cancel her visit? Naturally, she was delighted not to have to break into the precious day spent with Rob, though she was very curious to know the reason.

'I have friends coming down for the weekend, from London. They plan to stay in a local hotel and will spend both days with me. Make a nice change for me to have a visitor with me for a longer period.'

There was an implied criticism in his voice but she did not rise to the bait. She had been finding her visits growing more difficult as David's boredom was setting in and he became despondent about his future.

'How lovely for you. I hope you enjoy it. I'm sure Jamie will send his love and I'll explain to him why he won't be visiting.'

After she put the phone down, she was thoughtful. She didn't know he had friends in London who would be willing to spend a weekend in the area. All the same, it did mean that she, Rob and Jamie were now free to plan everything they wished.

As she predicted, Jamie was delighted that he did not have to make the awkward visit to his father. It was nearly the end of the school year and he was already making his own plans for an extended trip on the canal. He knew he would have to work hard on the adults if he was to get his way. He made up his mind to be as good as he possibly could, knowing that they would have to notice what a good influence the boat was. Cathy was curious at the change in him and wondered if he might be missing his father after all. She discussed it with Rob, once Jamie was in bed that evening.

'I guess he's up to something,' Rob admitted. 'But from what we know of him, it's unlikely. Now, do you think we could talk of something else, something other than Jamie or David? I'd like to talk about us, or not talk, as the case may be.'

He removed the wine glass from her long fingers and put it carefully down on the table. He pulled her hand to make her get up from her seat and led her to the futon seat at the side of the cabin.

'Now, there are more important things between us that we should think about. I have to admit that I have been giving them a lot of thought for the past few days.'

He got up again suddenly and crossed to his CD player. He put on a soft, romantic disc and the music flowed through the tiny cabin.

'Just making sure Jamie can't overhear,' he whispered.

'It's nice,' she whispered back. 'Now, what's so important?'

'This,' he said gently, taking her in his arms.

He pulled her close to him and she felt his warmth through her thin, cotton T-shirt. She sighed as she gave her kisses to him. He responded, his mouth soft against her own. He stopped kissing her for a moment and took her hand again, pulling her up from the seat.

'Let's go and look at the moon.'

Out on the deck, the night had fallen and the water sounds changed as different night creatures took over.

'What's that?' she asked, hearing a persistent rattling.

'Frogs,' he answered. 'There are dozens of them together, over in the next field. The tadpoles are all hatched now and they all have to try to find places to live. Look, there's the moon.'

The tiny sliver of light rose above the trees.

'You should wish on the new moon,' Rob told her, his arm warming her shoulders as they stood close. 'I've made my wish.'

Cathy sighed. It was so romantic, soft music drifting from the open cabin door, the moon, stars and a man with whom she was falling in love, holding her close.

'I've wished, but I'm not telling you what. It wouldn't come true, would it?'

'That depends. Cathy, is there no-one else who could look after Jamie? Grandparents? Aunts? Cousins?'

'No. His mother's parents completely lost touch, it seems, after their daughter died. David's an only child and his parents live in Australia. I've never heard anything of them at all, apart from Christmas and birthday cards, of course. But, here we are, talking about him again. I thought you wanted to talk about something else.'

'I want you to myself, for more than a short evening. I want us to travel on our own, to go out for meals together. Much as I love Jamie, I want to be with you for a while.'

'You've got me to yourself now,' she told him. 'That will have to do for the time being. Mind you, maybe when David is out of hospital, he can look after Jamie himself, at least for a few evenings.'

They went around in the usual circles, but it wasn't what either of them really wanted and her conscience would never allow her to abandon the boy or his father until some sort of future was settled.

'I wonder how David's getting on with his mysterious visitors,' Cathy said out aloud.

'Will we ever know?'

In his mind he added, or care. He

seriously wondered if they would ever progress beyond this stage.

Cathy sensed that Rob was getting tired of the situation and she even began to have doubts about spending so much time with him. She'd grown to rely on him, take him for granted, perhaps. His patience must be wearing a bit thin, she realised. She knew that she should do other things, besides centre her life around their weekend trips. She could not bear the thought of losing him, though. It was a problem for which she could see no solution, not yet.

After the weekend, she went to the hospital, hoping to see David in a more buoyant mood after his new visitors spending time with him. It seemed it had not been a success, however. He was unwilling to answer any of her questions and was morose and prickly. He seemed to have lost heart in doing anything and was very depressed.

'It seems they've decided to send me home quite soon. I shall have to attend physio sessions several times a week but at least I'll be home.'

'That must make you feel better,' she said brightly.

'I suppose so. At least I shall be able to see what Jamie's getting up to.'

Cathy had been continually speculating about what was to happen when David came out of hospital. He was going to need a great deal of care and support and she wasn't sure she was going to be able to manage. Neither was she sure how anything else could be organised.

As the time approached, she became restless and anxious. She really didn't want to spend the rest of her life working as David's unpaid nurse.

'You really ought to get on with your trip,' she said sadly to Rob, the day before David was due home. 'It isn't fair of us to keep you here. It isn't what you planned at all. Besides, I expect I shall be very busy over the next few weeks, until we know what is going to happen.'

'I thought you might like me to be around,' he replied, looking hurt.

'Of course I want you around, but there isn't much in it for you, is there? It's not going to be easy. I'm sure Jamie will want to be with his dad and I expect he'll need quite a lot of care. I suppose I shall have to stay on here and my free time will be sparse to say the least.'

Rob frowned. He removed his arm from her shoulders and rose from the sofa they'd been sharing.

'Are you trying to tell me to leave?' he asked.

'No, of course not, but David is hardly going to want another man sharing his home, even part-time. He's already very jealous of the relationship you have with Jamie. He always asks about his son and who is looking after him. I don't try to hide anything now. There's no point.'

'I'm glad to hear it, but I don't do anything special with Jamie. Just talk to him as one talks to anyone.'

'Perhaps that makes the difference. David never used to spend time with him, except for a few minutes before bedtime, and weekends, of course. Well, sometimes at weekends. But you, you've been a real friend to both of us and I thank you for it.'

'And now the man in your life is returning home. You no longer want me around. OK, I'll go. Been great knowing you.'

'Oh, Rob, you know it isn't like that.'

'Do I? I thought we'd become so much more than good friends.'

'We are. We have. Rob, I don't know how to explain. I simply don't think it's fair for me to keep you here when I don't know what's going to happen. And how can I abandon Jamie at this time? David needs him and he needs me. Of course I'd rather be with you, but how can I possibly leave?'

'Looks as if you have two clear choices. Cathy, I've fallen in love with you. I'd like to spend my time with you, all my time.'

'I think I love you, too. In fact, I'm sure I love you, but I don't see there are any clear choices. It's all too complicated. I love Jamie, very much, as if he were my own son. I can't possibly let him down. David certainly can't cope with him and probably he can't even cope with himself at present.'

'Marry me, Cathy,' Rob burst out suddenly.

'Marry you? But how can I?'

'Is it because you only think you love me? Don't you really love me enough?'

'Oh, Rob, yes, of course I do. But I can't leave Jamie. You know I can't, not just now.'

'I understand that, Cathy. I'm not asking you to leave them now, but you have to live a life of your own. What do you expect is going to happen? Do you plan to stay with David and Jamie until you become an old age pensioner? Perhaps I'd better leave you now. You need to do some clear thinking. I'll stay by the bridge for two more days to give you time to decide what you want to do, just the decision, not to take any dramatic action. If I hear nothing more from you by then, I shall move on and assume you have chosen David, instead of me. I'll stay until Thursday morning. That gives you two clear days and nights. If you don't come to see me, regretfully, I'll have to assume that it's all over.'

'Rob, please don't put me in this position. Don't make me choose between you, not right now. I might make the wrong choices.'

'Darling girl, I simply want you to think about your own future. I appreciate your loyalty to David and Jamie. It's a rare quality, but you must also think about yourself, unless it's David you really want and not me, of course. You can't give your life entirely to someone else's child, however adorable that child. I think I share many of your feelings about him. I just want to give you some space to make up your mind. Once you do, we can begin to plan for the future. If that future doesn't include me then that is your decision.'

He kissed the top of her head and went out of the room. She heard him slam the door as he left. That was it. Rob had gone. She might never see him again. She wept hot, bitter tears. It was an impossible situation. If he truly loved her, how could he do this to her? It simply wasn't fair.

After a while, she knew that she had to pull herself together. David was to return home the next morning and there were still masses of things she needed to get ready. It was fortunate that Jamie had slept through the evening. If he had heard any of her discussion with Rob, he'd be very upset to think he might not see him or his boat again. She couldn't believe it herself, if she was honest.

With a deep sigh, she set about her tasks before falling wearily into bed. If it was such a simple decision, she knew she would go and find Rob the very next day but she had responsibilities.

David arrived home in an ambulance

and a flurry of bad temper. Rob had previously helped Cathy to carry a bed downstairs and the dining-room had been turned into a sort of bed-sitting room for David. The downstairs shower room was to be his bathroom, for the time being. Thanks to intensive physiotherapy and plenty of support, he was now more or less able to get about on crutches. The early thoughts of him never walking again had been turned around and his prospects were looking very much better.

Unfortunately, his anger against the world hadn't changed and made him very difficult to live with. He blamed anyone and everyone for his predicament, though it had been made quite clear that the accident was entirely his fault. He was also about to face charges of drink driving. The doctors had warned him that he had to cut out all alcohol for the foreseeable future and much of the difficult time in hospital related to his sudden deprivation of drink.

While his medical prognosis was reasonably good, if he took care, his professional future was much less secure. Though they had been very sympathetic at his office, Maggie especially, once they had learned the full facts, they were slightly less enthusiastic to take him back. Maggie had fussed around the hospital on several occasions, bringing fruit and flowers, cards and, apparently, good wishes from everyone. Though David had been slightly mollified, he was still carrying a large chip on his shoulder about something.

As for the mysterious female client, girlfriend or whatever she was, there had been no sign, as far as Cathy knew. She had neither said anything to him about it nor asked questions. If David wanted to tell her, he would do so in his own time. Cathy did wonder about the visitor from London and if that might have been the same woman but if it was, then it was almost certainly over now.

It was also the start of the school holidays for Jamie, to add to the complications.

By the end of David's second day at home, Cathy was ready to jack in the whole business. She had been on the go the whole day, never stopping even to think. If it hadn't been for Jamie, she'd have dashed off to join Rob and sailed away into the proverbial sunset. With a stab of pain, she realised that Rob was due to sail into his own sunset, the very next morning. If she wanted to see him, it had to be right now, that evening. She took David's supper in to him and sat on a chair, preparing to talk. Before she could begin, however, David spoke.

'I'm sorry, Cathy. I've been a pig lately. I know you're unhappy, but I will try to make it up to you. I've been thinking, it would be a good idea if we got married. What do you say?'

'Married? You and me?'

Her voice shook. Once upon a time, she'd have almost dropped with pleasure at the suggestion. Now that she knew for certain that she loved Rob, it was the last thing in the world she wanted. She had sat down intending to tell him that she was going to meet Rob to tell him that she did want to marry him. Now this bombshell had hit her. David continued speaking.

'It seems like a good idea all round. You love Jamie and he loves you. You're such a competent lady, I'm sure we'd grow fond of each other in time.'

'Fond of each other?' she echoed in horror. 'You're talking about a marriage of convenience here. I know you don't love me and though I may be fond of you, I certainly don't love you.'

'You can't let me down, Cathy, not now. I really need you. I thought you cared for me. There was a time when I actually thought you wanted to be more than my employee. You do love Jamie though, you can't deny that, even if you don't think you love me.'

'I don't deny it, of course I love him. He's a dear little boy but I can't just marry you because I love your little son.

It's no basis for any sort of marriage. Now, I was planning to go out for a short time. I'll put Jamie to bed first, of course. I'm sure he'll be fine. If he needs anything, he's quite capable of coming down to see you.'

'You can't go, Cathy. I won't let you. Please don't leave us. I expect you intend to go and see your boyfriend, do you? You've changed, Cathy, become more selfish since you met him.'

She sighed and turned to leave.

His face took on an ugly expression and he almost snarled, 'Damn that man. It's him, isn't it? Clear out then. Go off with your bargee.'

He turned his face to the wall and allowed the tray of food to slip to the floor.

'David,' Cathy protested, 'your supper.'

'Damn supper. Damn everything. Leave me alone. Second thoughts, you can bring me a bottle of whisky here. Do you hear me?'

'I hear you but I won't, David. I won't bring you any alcohol,' she replied in a voice that was icily calm. 'You should know better than to ask. Haven't you learned anything? I'm going to put Jamie to bed now. I'll come back to clear away your mess later.'

She felt angry and trapped. David knew she was too fond of Jamie to leave him and was using it to blackmail her into staying. Her employer had become totally impossible and however understanding she tried to be, he was behaving outrageously. Once Jamie was asleep, she would go to Rob and tell him everything. She knew she wanted to promise to marry him if he was willing to wait just a little longer, until arrangements could be made for the care of both father and son.

She called Jamie to come for his bath and when he didn't come, she went to look for him. He was sitting in front of the television, his thumb stuck in his mouth.

'Come on, love. Bath-time.'

'I'm too busy.'

He continued to sit and suck his thumb.

'Since when did you start sucking your thumb again? You gave that up when you were five, remember?'

'Since you and Daddy started rowing all the time. I heard. You won't stay and live with us for ever, will you? You're going to leave us and go away with Rob.'

She tried to explain things but he couldn't or wouldn't see beyond the fact that she might leave them and very soon.

'You like Rob more than me.'

'I love you both, Jamie, but in different ways. You must understand that. Rob can't live here and I can't go and stay with him on his boat and stay here to look after you. Besides, you have got Daddy back home now. You must want to spend time with him.'

'He doesn't want to be with me. I'm just a nuisance, in everyone's way.'

He began to sob uncontrollably. Cathy put her arms round him to comfort him and held him close against her. She murmured small, comforting words as his sobs gradually subsided. Gently, she took him up to his bath and tried to make little jokes as she played water games with him until he seemed more his usual self.

As he went to bed, he asked if she would stay at home for the evening. He didn't want to be left with a bad-tempered invalid who didn't seem to want him around.

'I was just going out for a little while,' she said. 'Daddy's there. He's in his room if you want anything. I'm sure you'd be all right for just an hour or so.'

'Please, don't leave me, Cathy. I'm frightened.'

She sat by his bed until at last, he fell asleep. Though she hated leaving them, she knew that if she didn't go to see Rob this evening, she might lose him for ever. There could be no resolution but his ultimatum had left her feeling scared. If she didn't let him know she cared, he would leave the area and she might not find him again. She did always have his mobile phone number, she tried to convince herself, but it somehow wasn't enough. He wanted her commitment and she had to make it.

Quietly, she went downstairs and past the dining-room that was now David's room. She listened outside the door. He had his television on and seemed not to have heard her. She pulled on her fleece and opened the front door as quietly as she could, feeling like a prisoner trying to escape.

'Cathy?' David shouted.

She swore silently and turned back.

'Cathy, please come here. I'm sorry. Don't leave us, not tonight.

She sighed and turned back. She pushed open the door and went into his room.

'I'm so sorry,' he said. 'I don't mean to be so awful but it's so frustrating. I made a mess of things earlier and I want to put it right.'

'Can't it wait till tomorrow?' she hedged, desperately hoping she might still manage to see Rob as it was already almost nine.

'I don't think it can.'

It was almost as if he knew the whole situation was running out of time.

'I managed all that very badly. I'm sorry I dropped my tray. I'm sorry I upset you. But you have to realise what it's like for me. I'm not used to having people do things for me. I'm used to being in charge, controlling my life. I don't even know if I have a career left. Who is going to want an accountant who's a drunk?'

'You're being hard on yourself. You can cure the habit if you really want to.'

'But if I'm charged and found guilty, I shall end up in prison. What will happen to Jamie then?'

'I don't know,' she mumbled, realising that her own decisions were getting more difficult by the minute.

'Won't you think seriously about marrying me? Please, Cathy. We've always got on so well before all this happened. Couldn't you ever love me? Am I really such a terrible person?'

8

Cathy picked up the tray from the floor and the pieces of broken plate. The food was ruined and had made a mess on the carpet. Saying nothing, she left the room and returned with a bowl of water and cloth to wipe up the mess.

David watched as she worked, mumbling apologies. She returned a few minutes later with a sandwich and some coffee. Her mind was whirling and doing the small tasks gave her a few moments' respite. She had to find a way of telling David that she wouldn't marry him but without deflating his already fragile ego.

'You know I love Jamie. I couldn't love him more if he was my own. I may have thought I cared for you but I realise now that I don't, not in the way that would allow me to marry you. I'm fond of you, of course, but I could never be a second best for you.'

'I don't know what you mean,' he protested.

'Jamie's mother. I couldn't compete with her in your affections. You'll never love anyone like you loved Hazel.'

David stared down at his tray and finally raised his gaze to meet hers.

'Is that what you think? Cathy, Hazel was very far from the ideal wife. I did love her once but things changed. I tried to hold on to her when she didn't want to stay. She had never wanted a child and I foolishly insisted, thinking it might bring us closer.'

'But you always implied that she was so perfect.'

'I know. Call it misplaced loyalty to Jamie's mother, but we actually began to hate each other. She suffered badly from post-natal depression and began to drink when she couldn't cope any longer. We both ended up drinking far too much. One night, she stormed out after yet another blazing row and drove off the bridge and straight into the canal. She was killed instantly.'

'No wonder you didn't want Jamie to go anywhere near the water,' Cathy whispered, suddenly shocked.

'I've felt guilty ever since. If I hadn't argued, allowed her to drink so much . . . you name it, I've been there. There was also the question of whether or not she did it deliberately. As a result, Jamie was left alone with only an inadequate father. Her parents refused to see either of us again, obviously blaming me for her death and resenting the child that had driven her towards such a terrible fate.'

'I always thought you loved her too much, to even consider sharing your life with anyone else.'

'It was all my own guilt. I allowed it to ruin my life, and, yes, I admit I have been drinking too much recently. You're the only sane thing in my crazy life. You do understand why I need you so much, don't you?'

'I'm truly sorry, David. I do understand but it makes no difference. I still can't marry you.'

'But you would never be second best. Won't you consider it, not even for Jamie's sake?'

Cathy shook her head, and as she turned to go, she heard a noise from upstairs.

'Jamie,' she croaked, her voice hoarse from emotion.

She went to settle the little boy. He was barely awake but seemed to sense the tension in the house. Though he had been so tiny when his mother died, she wondered if his sensitivity to argument could have resulted from overhearing the rows of his parents.

'He's OK now,' she told David when she went down again.

He looked angry now, his eyes blazing with suppressed fury.

'If you won't marry me, then you might as well get off to your wretched boyfriend. I don't want you here. You can have notice. I can easily get someone else to look after the boy, and me, come to that.'

'I can't leave you like this, and Jamie, he will be terribly upset. He has no-one at this moment, except me and Rob, of course. But you have forbidden him to see Rob, haven't you?'

'You must now understand why.'

'I don't understand, of course, but you are forcing something on him for reasons that have nothing to do with him. He doesn't even realise why you don't want him to go near water. In any case, he can swim and the boat is completely safe, especially with the precautions we insist on taking.'

'What are you saying? You want to take Jamie away from me as well?'

'Oh, David, of course not, but you have to realise that you can't control everyone around you. You only want me because you're too scared I'll leave you with problems you can't handle. Marriage seems like the solution for you, but we'd end up hating each other. I have found you very difficult to live with the last few months. Jamie has responded to Rob because Rob spends time with him, listening to him, involving him in everything he does.'

'Then you'd better get off to see this paragon. I was serious. You can have notice to quit as soon as I find a replacement. I'll get on to an agency in the morning.'

With a sob of rage and frustration, she ran out of the room and upstairs. It was too late now to go to find Rob. He would be gone first thing and she couldn't possibly leave Jamie and David to cope on their own, not now. Jamie may be asleep but if he awoke, he'd need her. David would hear nothing, and if ever he insisted on having more to drink he could get it himself, crutches or no crutches.

She spent a restless night, tossing and turning and getting very little sleep. Several times she had almost got up to creep away and join Rob but the thought of the little boy asleep in the room next door made her stay. After breakfast, she took Jamie for a walk to the village to buy a few items they needed. She avoided all roads leading anywhere near the canal and would not talk about it to Jamie, whose persistent questions were making her feel even worse.

Eleven o'clock it was now. Rob would have left by now. She surreptitiously wiped away a tear, hoping Jamie hadn't noticed.

It was a long, dreary day. She had said little to David since his unexpected proposal and confidences and finally, his flurry of temper. He did have the good grace to look slightly ashamed of himself.

Once Jamie was in bed that evening, she told David she was going out for a walk. He nodded his agreement before asking her to leave the telephone within his reach.

She eventually stood by the bridge, their bridge, hers and Rob's. Ironic if it was the same one where David's late wife had lost her life. She shuddered at the thought. The towpath was empty. The Lady Barbara and its owner had gone. Wracked with sobs of unhappiness, she stared down at the still water. She had no doubt that she loved Rob but she had lost him. She had let him go. It was too late. She still had his phone number somewhere safe and knew that if things ever changed she might find the courage to use it.

* * *

Rob crept into her thoughts so many times during the days that followed. Whenever the phone rang, her heart pounded, but it was never for her. David was receiving an unusually large amount of personal calls, she realised, and he began to look more and more pleased with himself while she felt worse by the day. Surely Rob must ring. Surely he would want to know how she was. But there was nothing. She tried hard to forget him and for two long weeks, dragged herself through the chores.

'You're not much fun any more,'

Jamie complained. 'Is it 'cos of Rob?'

'I guess I am just tired, darling,' she replied. 'I have quite a lot to do, with Daddy needing so much looking after and now Mrs Morgan doesn't come any more, I have the cleaning to do as well.'

The lady who had been coming to clean the house had given up, partly because David had been upsetting her since his return and she had used the excuse of wanting to retire. There had seemed little anyone could do that pleased the man, but, Cathy had to admit, something was cheering him up, just over the last few days. She was puzzled — and intrigued.

'It's not fair at all,' Jamie moaned. 'Nobody cares about me. I wish I could go on Rob's boat with him, just us two on our own. Then nobody would have to fight and squabble.'

Cathy looked around, aware of movement behind her.

'David,' she said in surprise, seeing him standing against the door frame, leaning on his crutches. 'You're looking better. It's good to see you moving around a bit more.'

'You might like to take Jamie out for the day, go to the cinema or something, take him out for tea to a pizza restaurant or something. He isn't having much of a holiday. Do you both good.'

'Well, thanks, but how will you manage? I could leave something cold on a tray, I suppose. But what if you need help?'

'I have a sort of, well, a colleague is calling round. I'll be fine.'

Cathy supposed it would be Maggie and was immediately relieved.

'That will do you good. Great. We'll have us a bit of an outing, shall we, Jamie?'

'Yeah!' he yelled and bounced upstairs, excited that for once, something different was happening.

It took very little time for them to be ready to leave. Cathy put out various items of food for Maggie to prepare for

David and she left lists of instructions for him. He seemed impatient for her to leave.

'I think you're quite looking forward to having someone new to visit and fuss over you,' she teased. 'Maggie's such a good sort.'

He hesitated before speaking.

'Nonsense. I look forward to having someone different to talk to.'

All the same, she noticed that he had taken some trouble to smarten himself and was wearing one of his best shirts.

'You look smart,' she told him. 'Enjoy your visit.'

'I don't expect you back until late. Make sure you give the boy a good outing.'

Still feeling slightly puzzled at this sudden change in his attitude, she and Jamie set out for the town centre. It was a typical summer's day, cold, damp and drizzly!

'What do you want to do?' she asked him.

'Anything at all?'

'Within reason,' she allowed.

'Go skating, then go to the cinema and then go for a pizza. Dad said we could do anything.'

'OK,' she agreed.

David had indeed insisted they go out for a long time and enjoy themselves. That was exactly what she planned to do. When they got there, the skating rink was very full. The combination of school holidays and the wet day meant that the place was full of shouting children and exasperated parents. After a short time, Jamie was also feeling the pressure.

'It isn't so much fun when there are too many people, is it?' he shouted to her.

'Maybe there are some of your school friends here among the crowd.'

'I think I might have skated enough,' the little boy said seriously.

When they got outside, she could see that he was trembling slightly.

'I was a bit frightened,' he admitted. 'I like skating when we go and there is room to skate. Can we still go to the cinema?'

' 'Course we can. We'll get a huge tub of popcorn and scoff it all through the film. Now, let's decide what to see.'

There were several children's films showing for the holidays and she let Jamie choose what he wanted to see. It was unfortunate that the one he chose contained several scenes set on a narrow boat. Neither had known what the film was about but when she saw the brightly-painted boat, she had to stifle back the tears.

Jamie saw it quite differently and made comments about the way Rob would have done some things rather than as shown in the film. She barely saw the rest of the movie, her mind winging back to the lovely days they had shared with Rob. She closed her eyes, remembering his touch . . . his kiss and his kindness and idealism. Jamie nudged her hard.

'You're missing the best bits,' he hissed. 'Don't go to sleep.'

It was easier to let him think she was sleeping than try to explain how desperately she was missing the man she knew she had lost.

After a large pizza with everything on it, they finally set out for home. As they drove up to the house, a large sleek silver car was driving away.

'That doesn't look much like Maggie's car,' she muttered.

'It wasn't. Maggie's car is green and battered and that wasn't Maggie driving,' Jamie said.

'Did you see who it was?'

'Nah,' Jamie replied with a yawn. 'No-one important. Just some woman Dad knows.'

Cathy was intrigued and even more so when David insisted it had been Maggie visiting, or had he actually said it was Maggie? Maybe she had simply assumed it was Maggie. She remembered the mysterious woman he had been meeting that fateful day of the accident. It could have been her perhaps.

When she saw David, he looked slightly flushed, she thought, and wondered if he had been drinking again. She did not even ask. After a pleasant time away from the house with Jamie, she didn't feel like any confrontations. He did not want a meal, saying he'd eaten with his visitor. He was still looking unusually pleased with himself and Cathy stared at him curiously. She took Jamie upstairs to get him into bed. He was obviously tired out.

'Thanks, Cathy. That was great. That film really made me want to go on Rob's boat again, though. Do you think we can?'

'I'm not sure. Maybe, one day, but Rob's left now. We don't know where he is.'

'You still have his mobile number haven't you?' he said with a sly grin.

'I might have. Time for sleep now.'

'I still think you should ring him,' the child called out softly, so his father couldn't hear.

She went to bed early, partly to give

herself time to think and also because she didn't really want to talk to David. She knew he had spent the day with someone other than his secretary and if he wanted to fib about it, that was up to him. All the same, it was good to see him looking a bit more cheerful and it certainly lessened the pressure on her.

'I've been thinking. You and Jamie need a holiday,' David said surprisingly the next day. 'I can arrange for someone to come in to get meals for me once or twice a day. After yesterday, I realise it's time I began to take control of things again. I spent the whole night thinking and planning. I'm sorry I have been such a dreadful misery for so long.'

'It certainly hasn't been easy but it's understandable,' Cathy replied, still puzzled — and intrigued — by the change in David.

'It seems I'm not a total failure after all. This friend of mine, a client, well, I have come to know her well in the past few months, very well.'

He paused, looking embarrassed.

'But about you and Jamie. You could go to the seaside. Jamie will like that.'

'Maybe. If you really think you can manage. What brought this on?' she asked, but he ignored her question.

'Or you may prefer to join your friend on his boat. I know Jamie would like that even more.'

'Why this sudden change of heart?'

David shrugged and looked away.

'But it's too late. He's left the area,' she added.

'I thought you said he had a mobile phone,' David persisted.

'He does but I foolishly let him leave when I'd promised to meet him. He'd have known that if I didn't turn up, I wouldn't go away with him. Maybe he won't want to see me again.'

'Go on, call him. I can see you want to. If he says no, at least you will be certain.'

'Oh, David, do you mean it? You can let me go?'

Her eyes filled with tears of joy. If

Rob really loved her, he would wait for her. This time, she would not hesitate.

'But how will you manage? Who'll look after you?'

'I have been speaking to my, er, my friend.'

'Doesn't she have a name?' Cathy asked impatiently.

'Jennifer. Jennifer Ward. She's a widow. We were actually seeing each other regularly for a time. I helped her to organise her finances after her husband's death, some time ago, and we kept in touch. I thought she wouldn't want anything more to do with me, after the accident, but it seems she doesn't mind. She thinks she'll be able to cope and insists that I'll soon be walking again. She's coming over again, later. Now, why don't you go and try to contact your Rob?'

'But you are still going to need a lot of help for the next few weeks. And what about the future? How will you manage with Jamie?'

'I think Jennifer will get on well with

him. She's really a lovely person, very patient and she's always wanted children. When her husband died, she thought she'd lost her chance, and long term, well, Jamie will be going to boarding school in a couple of years. I have always planned for that, as you know. I couldn't expect you to stay here for ever. You need to find your own life, I realise that now. If things work out as we hope, Jennifer and I will be here for the holidays and perhaps Jamie can come to see you sometimes. I take it Rob is serious about you, wants more than friendship from you.'

'He wanted to marry me, and I desperately want to marry him if he'll still have me. It's all up in the air really.'

'Then you'd better see if you can find him. Cathy, I am very grateful to you, for everything you've done, and your loyalty. I apologise once more for my dreadful behaviour and total selfishness. And as for my marriage proposal, that was an act of desperation, I suppose. I hope you don't hold that against me.'

'Of course not, David. It was just a bit of a shock at the time, so unexpected. I'll always be very fond of you, and I admit that, once, I'd have been over the moon if you'd shown any interest in me. But that was before I met Rob.'

'I hadn't realised things were so serious with Rob. I was very rude about him, slightly jealous perhaps, of both you and Jamie. He seemed able to get on better with my son that I could. I really do wish you well, every happiness.'

'And I wish the same for you, David.'

He reached for her and they hugged each other then he pushed her away and nodded towards the telephone, smiling. Still amazed at his words, without any further hesitation, she rushed into the hall and dialled Rob's number. He answered at the first ring.

'Oh, Cathy, thank heavens. I was about to call you. Telepathy, isn't it? I'll give you just half an hour to get yourself down to the bridge. After that, I really shall leave.'

'What bridge? I thought you'd already left, ages ago.'

'I did leave, but I came back. How could I go anywhere without my favourite crew? The boat seemed so empty without you. I love you, darling. Please say you'll come to me.'

'I'll be back to collect my stuff and Jamie later,' she told David once she'd hung up, then she ran all the way to the bridge, to Rob's waiting arms.

'I do love you, so very much,' she whispered, as they kissed.

'I was so scared you wouldn't come back to me, and I don't intend to make you live on a boat all our lives. This is temporary, until we finish exploring the wet bits of Britain.'

'There are a lot of wet bits. I hope it takes quite a long time.'

'We can take all the time we need.'

A kingfisher darted among the trees. They caught their breath and watched the tiny bird as it skimmed the water.

'It's so lovely,' Cathy said softly.

'Like you,' Rob whispered, his arms firmly around the woman he loved so much.

THE END